His touch was
subtle seduction . . .

his lips were gentle, the softness of his mustache a velvet brush. The quick path of his tongue across her lower lip sent a shivery need through Jennifer's entire body.

With an urgency she'd never before experienced, Jennifer opened to the gentle penetration of Grady's tongue. He intensified the kiss, probing, exploring, demanding a response that she gave in equal measure. He claimed her lips, her mouth, her very soul. Conquered, she offered no resistance.

The rest of the world faded away like meaningless props on an empty stage. Indelibly, the warmth of his arms branded her through the cotton of her dress. His lips seared their shape and texture into her memory.

Only one thought was imprinted in her mind: Grady Murdock really was a modern-day villain.

ABOUT THE AUTHOR

For Charlotte Maclay, the newspaper, a little article buried inside, or the people she knows are an unending source of ideas. The inspiration for *The Villain's Lady* came after she and her husband visited a small town in California. The evening's entertainment was a local melodrama, and Charlotte immediately began to think what fun it would be if the heroine fell in love with the villain. This is Charlotte's first Harlequin American Romance novel.

CHARLOTTE MACLAY

THE VILLAIN'S LADY

Harlequin Books

TORONTO • NEW YORK • LONDON
AMSTERDAM • PARIS • SYDNEY • HAMBURG
STOCKHOLM • ATHENS • TOKYO • MILAN
MADRID • WARSAW • BUDAPEST • AUCKLAND

To Chuck, for his inspiration,
with thanks to all of my friends in RWA

Published February 1993

ISBN 0-373-16474-2

THE VILLAIN'S LADY

Chapter One

Grady Murdock wheeled his sleek Porsche to a stop next to a split-rail barricade. As a cloud of floury dust settled on the black-mirror finish of the car, a scowl tightened his forehead.

Getting out, he loosened his tie and unbuttoned his starched collar. Dragging the tie from around his neck, he let it dangle loosely from his hand. He walked with long, confident strides down the middle of the dirt street.

A dog the size of a small horse ambled up beside him and snatched the tie from his fingers. He loped easily away down the center of the dirt street.

"Hey! Gimme back my tie!" Grady shook his fist at the dog. The thief looked like a cross between a St. Bernard and a German shepherd, all molasses brown and shaggy.

Jaw clenched, Grady took off in pursuit of the four-legged bandit.

A youngster rolling a wooden hoop dashed in front of him. Grady took a startled step out of the way as two other children raced pell-mell after the first, a black and white terrier yapping at their heels. The girl's long dress swayed energetically, her bloomers visible with each step, her bonnet bouncing at her back. The boys wore overalls with homespun shirts.

Grady stared after the youngsters feeling distinctly as though he'd been dropped into the middle of a children's history book. Annoyed, he wondered what the heck was going on.

Someone was either videotaping a nostalgic piece for "Little House on the Prairie," or the restored Sierra mining town of Moraine had done one terrific job recreating the past. The clapboard buildings looked like they'd each received a new coat of paint. With some clever illusion, the air seemed fresher within the boundaries of the town than it had on the highway, and the summer sky looked brighter.

The few people walking down the street or talking in groups along the boardwalk were in costume, including a Chinese fellow with a braided queue down his back.

Puzzled, Grady slowed his pace.

Was he the only tourist in town? Grady wondered as he purposefully tracked the tie-carrying dog down the center of the dusty street. He considered giving up the chase. The tie, dragging through the fine, gritty dirt was likely to be a total loss. It was one of his favorites, though.

The dog, resembling a Behemoth from the past, skirted the saloon and another group of costumed locals, then checked over his shoulder as though making sure Grady was still on his tail. Apparently satisfied, he trotted through the stage door of Moraine Theater. According to the hand-painted sign, the weathered building had been the Home of Summer Melodramas since 1870.

After the bright sunshine, the musty darkness backstage disoriented Grady. As his eyes adjusted to the dimness, he noted overhead lighting racks hanging at oddly canted angles. The stage itself was made of rough planks worn smooth and shiny. Along the front edge of the stage, oil lanterns were set to illuminate the play in the old-fashioned way. Stacked sets leaned against the back wall in a jumble.

The short hairs along the back of Grady's neck rose to attention, a cold draft circling around him. The place felt haunted. The faint scent of greasepaint and the echo of laughter lingered in the air.

He shook his head to dislodge uncharacteristic thoughts of ghosts. A man with an M.B.A. wasn't supposed to give himself over to images of spirits raised from the dead.

But where the hell had that dog gone with his tie? That creature had certainly been flesh and blood.

Out of the shadows a vision appeared. She wore a pastel blue dress that skimmed the floor and had a tapered waist he could circle with his hands. A modest white collar managed to emphasize her graceful neck, and hair the color of golden sunbeams on a summer day cascaded down her back. Full, sensuous lips smiled from a heart-shaped face, and innocent blue eyes questioned him.

Clutching the silk tie her dog had delivered to her, Jennifer Sweetham stared at the stranger standing center stage. Her breath lodged uncomfortably in her throat. The man was the image of self-confidence. Broad-shouldered, lean of hip, with legs that seemed to go on forever, he dominated the stage by the sheer force of his presence. If he wasn't an actor he certainly should be. Without speaking a single line he already had her anxious for his autograph—and maybe a whole lot more.

Her dog had fetched her a real prize this time.

Watching the woman approach, Grady's internal warning system went to full alert. Certain other parts of his anatomy leapt unexpectedly to a stand-by mode.

"Were you looking for this?" she asked. Her melodious voice was like velvet, draping itself over his skin. From her hand hung his battered tie. The same way an afternoon sun dances across the San Francisco Bay, amusement sparkled in her eyes, bemusing and subtly hypnotic.

Struggling against her mesmerizing effect, he said, "The dog stole my—"

"I am sorry. Bonbon doesn't usually misbehave like that."

"That huge animal? Bonbon?"

She lifted her delicate shoulders. "I suppose he's outgrown the name a bit."

"I'd classify that as an understatement."

She smoothed his tie with little success, except the movement of her slender fingers across the fabric seemed to vibrate along Grady's back instead, unnerving him with its sinuous motion. This was some kind of woman, sexy as hell without even trying.

"I guess I should offer to buy you a replacement." She studied the rumpled silk with an arched eyebrow. "Though this one really is quite dull. Maybe we could find something more interesting at the mercantile."

"You don't have to do that." Their fingers brushed as he took the tie and shoved it into his pocket. Heat arrowed up his arm and slammed into his chest. He swallowed dryly. "My name's Murdock. Grady Murdock."

For an instant the flicker of alarm flared in her incredibly blue eyes. Fear? Of him? That hardly seemed possible.

"Of course," she said, visibly regaining her composure. "You're perfect! Absolutely perfect. A casting director's dream." Her light laughter echoed around the empty stage and lapped infectiously against Grady's heart, doing a hell of a number somewhere around his gut, too. "I should have known."

"Known what?"

"Even your mustache is perfect." Jennifer's hand moved as though to touch the attractive dark brush above his lips. Lord, she hadn't expected to find Grady Murdock on her stage, or that he'd be a six-foot hunk of solid masculinity. She was going to have to do some very fast talking. "Could be a bit longer at the tips, I suppose, but quite stylish and natural. A perfect villain."

Her gesture startled Grady. Had she really touched him? Or had he only imagined the intimate warmth of her slender fingers? It was the sexiest gesture he'd ever seen, yet her movements were only an illusion and seemed totally innocent. Maybe.

"Villain?" Grady covered his surprise while wondering if she had mistaken him for someone else. He'd always thought of himself as the hero type, at least when it came to beautiful women.

"Twirl your mustache for me. Please."

For a woman this beguiling, he was willing to play a whole lot of games. Eventually they'd find some interesting ones they could play together.

He twisted the end of his mustache between his thumb and finger. "Like that?"

"Spectacular. Now sneer for me." Laughter threatened to muffle her words.

Cocking his head and letting his gaze slowly peruse the delicate column of her neck and the soft swell of her breasts, he declined. "I make it a point not to sneer at lovely ladies."

"Go ahead," she urged with an irresistible smile, a dimple appearing in her cheek. "Lift one side of your mouth. Just your upper lip." He did as she asked and she clapped her hands, laughing again. "Wonderful! You're hired."

The stage seemed to shift beneath his feet. What kind of enchanted place was Moraine that had him so off balance? Or was this woman simply a bewitching sorceress. "Who are you and what did you just hire me to do?"

As easily as water slipping over a dam, she linked her arm through his and managed to tie his heart in knots at the same time. "I'm Jennifer Sweetham, of course. Director of Moraine Theater summer melodramas."

"Also the heroine?" Grady asked, even though the wide bow at the back of her head was a dead giveaway.

"Naturally. Along with stage manager, ticket taker, set painter and general roustabout. I've just hired you to be the villain. What else?"

"I don't think—"

"Don't be shy. Central casting has done me a real favor." She ushered him outside and he had the feeling he was being led through a door he'd been avoiding for years. "Let me show you the cabin where you'll be staying. You'll have to leave your car parked outside of town but it's not a long walk. Rehearsal's at seven tonight."

"I really think you must have me confused with someone else."

"You're an actor, aren't you? I can hear it in your voice. A singer, too?"

Her question brought a flash of memory. The excitement of his moment on stage. Bright lights. Makeup caking his face. Applause. The youthful dream that had him briefly considering an acting career. A fantasy long ago forgotten.

"I once played the lead in a high school musical," he admitted dryly.

Jennifer laughed as though he'd just told the most marvelous joke in the world. "You see? I knew I was right." Thank goodness, she thought. If he hadn't ever done any acting she would never be able to get away with the plan that was just now forming in her mind.

A thoroughly desperate plan, she admitted, keeping a friendly smile on her face.

Grady walked beside her, liking the way she clung so comfortably to his arm. He didn't understand what was going on, but he wasn't crazy enough to object. The sensation of her closeness was heady, along with the sweet scent of her perfume. Violets, he thought. The scent was likely to keep him awake all night.

"Maybe I should try out for the hero's part. Then I'd get the girl."

"Oh, no. You're definitely the villain type. Dark hair. Wicked eyes. And your marvelous mustache." She lifted the hem of her skirt and stepped gracefully off the boardwalk onto the street. The guy might be the best looking man Jennifer had ever seen, with arms that were rock solid, but if he had a villain's heart, she and all of Moraine were in deep trouble.

Following Jennifer's lead, Grady had the odd sensation he'd come into the middle of a Western movie and had found himself on the screen. Glancing at his feet, he half expected to see cowboy boots. He supposed he ought to swagger, just a little.

The massive dog lumbered up beside Grady to provide additional escort service. The animal's tongue lolled moistly from side to side.

"I really hadn't planned to stay in Moraine," Grady insisted, torn between asserting himself and simply enjoying the improbable situation.

"Of course you will. When we have out-of-town performers we always put them up in one of Aunt Nyla's cabins. No charge."

"That's very kind of you but I already have reservations in Sonora." When he confidently named the three-check motel, the best available in the neighboring town, she wrinkled her upturned nose.

"That's so boring," she said. "It's like every other motel in the world. Besides, you won't be able to get any rest with all that road noise. You'll sleep much better here in Moraine. I promise you."

Interesting promise, Grady mused, wondering if Jennifer Sweetham would be willing to assure him a pleasant night's rest on a personal basis. Not that he'd get much sleep at all if he could entice her to share either a motel room or a cabin in the woods.

When he spotted the clapboard cabins across the road, he winced inwardly and understood why Aunt Nyla wouldn't charge for visitors. *Rustic* was another one of those understatements. The sight was not encouraging. He generally went first-class.

"The cabins originally housed some of the mine workers," Jennifer explained. "Mostly foremen and their families. The workers were rarely married."

"I can understand that."

"The cabins really are quite comfortable."

He felt the defensive tension in her arm. "I don't suppose there's anyplace to plug in my laptop computer."

"All the cabins have electricity, for heaven's sake. But why anyone would want to waste this lovely scenery just to sit in front of a computer is beyond me." She guided him toward the most isolated of the five tiny cabins, one flanked by lodge pole pines and boasting a porch with a wooden swing.

"Look, I really think there's been some kind of mistake," Grady began. He'd lost control of the situation and needed to get back in charge. Forget how intriguing visions of Jennifer sharing his cabin kept popping into his head.

A youngster resembling a tiny Tom Sawyer flew at them from down the path. He wore overalls and sported a floppy hat perched on the back of his head.

"Mom! I found one! He's a giant," the child insisted, his bare feet sliding to a stop in front of Jennifer. About six years old, his curly hair was the same sunbeam shade as his mother's.

"What is it you found, Danny?"

He carefully held up a lizard for his mother's dutiful inspection. A grin split the child's face, revealing one missing tooth.

"My gracious! He is beautiful, isn't he?" She stroked the creature's head with a single finger and crooned an endearing phrase.

"He's gonna win, Mom. I know he is."

"He certainly looks healthy enough," she agreed.

"The lizard's going to win what?" Grady asked.

Jennifer glanced up at him again, with those glorious blue eyes that made his groin muscles tighten and his head swim with erotic messages. "The race, of course. Some towns have frog-jumping contests. We have a lizard race."

He nodded. Somehow he should have known.

"We also have hoop-rolling contests, mumblety-peg events, horse races down the center of Main Street, and we auction off picnic lunches made by all the single women in town. The big event is in two days. After that we open the town for the tourists."

"Sounds like a whole lot of excitement. It's a wonder anybody survives."

Her forehead pleated into a frown, surprisingly intense and determined. A frown Grady had the strangest urge to smooth away with his fingertips. Or, better yet, with his lips.

"It's considerably more fun than getting stuck in rush-hour traffic, and it keeps the kids away from TV and drugs, which is more than I can say for what goes on in most big cities."

"Whoa." He held up a hand in self-defense. "I didn't mean to insult you or your town."

Her eyes narrowed and she gazed at him suspiciously.

"Mom, what'll I do with my lizard? I gotta keep him till the race." Danny tugged on his mother's long skirt.

Cupping the back of the boy's head affectionately, Jennifer said, "Why don't you take him home? I bet

Aunt Nyla has a shoe box that would make a perfect house for him.''

"Cute kid," Grady commented as the boy made a mad dash toward a two-story house not far from the cottages.

"My pride and joy."

"And your husband's, too, I imagine."

Without looking away from her son's flight, Jennifer softly said, "No husband."

"Ah, I see. You're the Widow Sweetham. Every town needs a sweet, innocent widow for the local men to protect." He'd read his share of Western novels. That also meant she was available. For him.

She turned slowly, lifting her chin to gaze at him levelly. The sparkle had vanished from her eyes. "I'm more like the 'fallen woman' and I assure you, I don't need any protection in this town. These people are all my friends."

Grady shoved his hands in his pockets, wishing he could also manage to take his foot out of his mouth. Tactless comment. He hadn't meant to offend her. In fact, he immediately missed the diamond sparkle that had vanished from her eyes. "No offense," he mumbled. He wasn't usually quite so tongue-tied around a woman.

But Jennifer Sweetham was significantly different from any female he'd ever met . . . and far more alluring.

Not that it mattered, he told himself resolutely. He was here to take care of business in Moraine, and then he'd be on his way.

The fact that he wanted to drag this beautiful, guileless woman into his arms and feel her delicate body along the length of his was unimportant. An aberration brought on by the strange, otherworldliness of the town. A tugging, aching need he'd never before experienced. A force he could easily resist.

If he wanted to.

Which he didn't.

His arm reached out to circle her slender waist and he pulled her close. "I'd like to be your friend, too." And a whole lot more.

Jennifer let out a startled gasp.

Like an overgrown puppy, Bonbon raised himself on two legs, rested his paws comfortably on Grady's shoulder and licked his face. The animal's breath was hot and reeked of doggy biscuit, jolting Grady back to some sense of reality.

Jennifer visibly stifled a laugh. "Moraine's a very friendly town."

"I can see that." His eyes teared from the dog's breath. Reluctantly he released his grip on Jennifer's waist and lifted the animal's paws from his shoulder. "And you're well chaperoned."

"Bonbon wouldn't hurt a fly."

"Just lick him to death."

Again her laughter, as light and airy as a mountain stream cascading over a rock-strewn path, swept past Grady's heart. He wanted to catch and bottle the sensation. It'd be worth a fortune.

"I have to make sure Danny doesn't terrorize Aunt Nyla with his lizard," she announced. "You just let yourself into the cabin. The door's open. Get settled and I'll see you at seven.''

She whirled away, her skirt billowing like a blue cloud, and he caught a fleeting glimpse of shapely ankles.

"No, wait!" he called after her, fighting her bewitching effect. "I can't act."

Heedless of his words she vanished along the narrow path that led to the larger house.

Grady was tempted to follow. He really shouldn't let her go on believing he was an actor. Where on earth had she gotten that idea? And why hadn't he been able to correct the notion? Jennifer Sweetham was strangely difficult to talk to, and ever so pleasant to be near.

Deciding he'd have to deal with the misunderstanding later, Grady turned back toward the center of town. He shoved his hand into his pocket and jingled a few coins. His silver dollar lucky piece was there where it belonged. A comforting feeling. His father had given him the coin when he was seven, and Grady had vowed never to spend it.

A horse-drawn wagon filled with beer barrels passed him on the street and stopped in front of the saloon. Two young girls played jacks on the boardwalk next to the mercantile. In an alley between two buildings, boys were pitching pennies against a wall.

Grady knew he'd really stepped back in time when he found the door to the bank locked. The lettering on the window announced the bank was open ten to three, weekdays. No late afternoons or evenings for the convenience of the customers. No ATM. Not even a night deposit.

Irritated, he wondered how anyone could expect to run a successful business that way. He could almost hear his father echoing the same sentiment from his grave.

JENNIFER PACED the length of Aunt Nyla's kitchen and back again. Her black shoes tapped an agitated beat on the linoleum floor.

Matching her step for step, Nyla kept trying to force an amber glass of chilled lemonade into her hands. The older woman's spectacles were perched on top of her white hair and her cheeks were flushed.

"I can't believe what I just did," Jennifer complained, finally pausing by the kitchen sink. She bent over the tile counter and carefully removed her contact lenses, placing them in a small container.

"Are your eyes bothering you again, dear?" Nyla asked.

"It's all the pollen in the air this time of year. My eyes itch and tear like crazy if I don't take the contacts out every few hours." She turned to her aunt who was now slightly out of focus.

"And it always seems worse when you're upset. Surely things aren't as bad as you think."

"You don't understand. He was right there. In the theater. Our real-life villain who's going to foreclose on the whole town, and all I could do was laugh. He must think I'm a total ninny."

Nyla managed to press the glass into Jennifer's hand. "No one would think that of you, dear. You're really quite bright."

"I certainly didn't handle the situation very well with Mr. Murdock." She nodded her thanks to the woman who had raised her. A quintessential grandmother type, her Great-Aunt Nyla had the ample breasts and comfortable lap perfect to cuddle a lonely child whose parents had died. No one would guess by her appearance that Nyla supplemented her modest income by writing bitingly funny greeting card verses.

"I do suppose it wasn't a good idea for you to laugh at him," Nyla conceded.

"Oh, I wasn't really laughing *at* him. Just at the irony of the situation." The icy tartness of the lemonade calmed her slightly. Grady Murdock's appearance on her stage had been thoroughly disconcerting. There'd been something about the way he'd looked at her, his gaze skimming her with blatant masculine approval, which had been quite unnerving. She'd barely been able to think clearly and still felt shaken.

He was a villain, she sternly reminded herself. Granted, a wickedly handsome one, but no doubt closely related to the devil himself.

"We heard this morning that Grady Murdock was coming to the mountains, probably to foreclose on the loan," Jennifer explained. "The town council had an emergency session and the only plan we could come up with was to find a way to get him to stay in town long enough to understand what we're trying to do here."

"Get him to fall in love with our homespun ways?" Nyla asked.

"That was the idea. Then he appeared right on my stage." She laughed again at her own audacity. "Nyla, I can't tell you how much he looks like the 'evil Pierre' in our melodrama, except maybe far more handsome than a villain deserves. And there he was, planning to figuratively toss us all out in the cold, just like any good villain would do. And I was supposed to get him to stay in town for a while. So I offered him the part."

"Oh, dear." Nyla's eyelids fluttered in surprise and her pale blue eyes widened. "I wouldn't think a banker would make a very good actor."

"He's not really a banker, but something close to it, I think." Agitated, she ran her fingertips up and down her glass, leaving damp paths through the condensation. She could still see the dark shadow of his afternoon beard and his eyes gazing at her. As thoroughly villainous as he might appear, her hands had itched to palm his cheeks, to experience the feel of his rough whiskers, the thrill of touching the rugged angles and planes of his face.

"And actually, he'd be wonderful in the part," she said, ignoring the almost physical sensation brought on by her wayward thoughts. "His voice projects beautifully. Very deep. Very sexy." She also recalled the way the corners of his eyes crinkled when he smiled and how parenthetical lines formed deliciously around his mouth. Very appealing and quite compelling.

"Really?" Curious, Nyla gave Jennifer's hand a little squeeze. "He must have made quite an impression on you. I haven't heard you call a man sexy in a long time."

"I didn't mean it that way. Purely in a theatrical sense."

"Of course."

Jennifer swallowed the denial that came to her lips. Her great-aunt had always been a very perceptive woman. "Anyway, now I don't know what to do. I was just thinking on my feet when I offered him the part. It was the only idea that came to mind." And her thought processes at that particular moment were clearly suspect. She'd suddenly been obsessed with images of moonlit nights and hot, sweaty bodies.

"Jake Tyson won't be all that pleased to lose the part to some total stranger from San Francisco."

"I know. But it would only be for a few days. Over the weekend, if we can get Murdock to stay that long . . . and if I can really convince him he's a natural-born villain with the world as his stage."

"Seems to me the only way to convince anything to someone like a banker is to talk money."

"I suppose you're right. Though that seems so crass." She downed another gulp of lemonade, her tension making her swallow with difficulty. "Meanwhile I think I've totally confused the man. He tried so hard to tell me he wasn't an actor and I refused to listen. I didn't dare until it was after three and I knew the bank would be closed. Marty had seemed so upset when he called the emergency meeting, I was sure he'd be a nervous wreck if Murdock showed up in his office.''

"Marty, sweet as he is, prefers to have his life scripted rather than trying to ad-lib," Nyla agreed. Her eyes twinkled with secret mirth and a little smile played at the corners of her lips.

"True enough. But now I'm going to have to make up some absurd story if we're going to get away with this charade." With any luck at all, she would avoid letting Grady know just how much he'd affected her.

"You're very creative, dear. I'm sure you'll think of something."

Nyla had always had enormous faith in her niece. Sometimes, like now, Jennifer wasn't at all sure it was warranted. But as a member of the town council, she had to do what she could to prevent the foreclosure. If the investors would just give them a little more time . . .

Her mind shifted to Grady Murdock, and the long, hard length of his body when he'd pulled her close. For a moment she'd been feverishly aware of his masculinity, his musky male scent and the determined glint in his dark eyes.

He was definitely a dangerous man, dangerous to the town and to a woman's peace of mind. With one smoky look he'd effortlessly set her nerves jumping and tangling around each other; something she hadn't felt in a very long time.

GRADY HEFTED his suitcase into the homey, pine-paneled cabin.

In the bedroom he discovered a double bed covered with a handmade quilt in an intricate floral design. The single blanket was one hundred percent wool, meant to ward off the chill of mountain nights. He fingered the down soft blanket. Beneath her old-fashioned costume, he imagined Jennifer's flesh would feel like satin and be far more effective than any blanket to keep a man warm.

Perhaps there were some advantages to staying in Moraine instead of a sterile motel in the neighboring town.

That thought brought a predatory smile to his lips. Capturing Jennifer, her inviting mouth, the soft swell of her breasts and the narrow width of her waist, would make any guy a successful big game hunter. But no way would he keep that kind of trophy mounted over his fireplace.

Putting the thought aside for the moment, he changed into slacks and a cotton sport shirt, then investigated the cabin more closely. There wasn't much to see.

A basket of fresh fruit in the refrigerator tempted him. Selecting a red apple, he polished it on his sleeve. Nice friendly touch, he thought.

Tossing the apple lightly in his hand, he strolled out the door onto the porch.

Something black and white and very quick leapt into the air and snatched the apple from his hands.

"Son of a gun!" The whole town was filled with thieves!

The creature darted away from the cabin. It ran with a lopsided gait heading directly for the larger house up the hill.

It figured Jennifer would have a raccoon for a pet. A nice match for a racing lizard and a dog the size of Secretariat.

Shaking his head, Grady trudged up the path toward her house, its steeply sloping roof and rough wood siding visible through the pines.

Spotting Jennifer standing next to a wire cage at the back of the house, Grady was struck by a whole array of uncharacteristic thoughts—Mom's apple pie, family picnics on the Fourth of July, Christmas carols around the tree—all things he'd seen on nostalgic postcards but never experienced in real life.

Now why would his mind fill with those images? he wondered. Granted, he'd known a fair number of beautiful women in his thirty-plus years, but none had conjured up fireworks and marching bands in his head. Jennifer managed to present an extraordinary picture just doing ordinary things.

That was it, he decided, some kind of reverse psychology. In her old-fashioned costume, with a long skirt and puffy sleeves, everything was left to his imagination. Which had swung into high gear at the same time he developed a sudden complaint about the fit of his slacks across his thighs.

Maybe it was the altitude. Oxygen deprivation.

Or maybe it was the sun-kissed skin of her arms, golden and soft and inviting. Or the tumble of hair down her back. Or the way he wanted to make her laugh again so her dimple would show.

His stride lengthened.

She turned slowly toward him, a column of afternoon sunlight backlighting her hair, making it shimmer with mellow warmth. In her arms she carried a pan of cut apples and oranges.

Grady's slacks seemed to shrink another full size.

"I think your friend has been snacking before dinner," he said with a smile.

She gave him a puzzled look.

"Your raccoon."

"Zorro?"

"Ah, the masked bandit." The culprit rattled up on top of his cage and peered down at them. He daintily bit into Grady's apple. "He filched the apple right out of my hand."

"Oh, dear." Her dimple appeared as if by magic and Grady knew he would have sacrificed a bushel of apples just for her smile.

"I've changed the bolt mechanism on his cage three times," she explained, "and he always figures out how to work it. I guess I'll have to put a padlock on it."

"Don't make it a combination lock," Grady warned. "He probably reads numbers."

She laughed and opened the cage door. "Come on, Zorro. You and Bonbon have embarrassed me enough for one day."

He watched the graceful way Jennifer moved, the delicate curve of her back and how the sun turned her hair to glistening threads of gold.

With an effort he cleared the lump in his throat and tried to ignore another, much more achingly uncomfortable sensation lower in his body.

"Look, Jennifer, I have a confession to make."

Chapter Two

This is it, Jennifer thought, feeling an anxious flutter in her stomach. He was going to tell her he wasn't an actor. This time she'd have to listen. And then think of something—quick.

"I'm sorry there's been this misunderstanding," Grady began, his deep voice resonant in the quiet woods. "I represent Sierra Syndications, the investors in Moraine."

She widened her eyes in her most surprised expression. "But I'd called a casting agency in Los Angeles. They said they would try to send someone for the part. You're so perfect I just assumed . . ."

He smiled in a rakish way and Jennifer's heart did a quick two-step. "You were wrong, I'm afraid."

Bonbon appeared from the far side of the house. He nuzzled up next to Jennifer and she petted him distractedly, measuring her words with the care of an Oscar-winning script writer.

"If you weren't sent by the casting office, and nobody else has shown up, then I don't know what we're going to do." She let a troubled expression cross her face. "Our regular villain, ah, broke his leg. If we can't open the show this weekend we won't be able to cover any of our costs."

"Including the mortgage?"

"Most especially that. It's such a shame. I imagine your investors will be quite upset." Warming up to the scene, she recalled how she'd always loved improvisation. She'd better do a convincing job now or all of her dreams for Moraine would collapse disastrously.

"The town's already well behind in their payments."

"Yes, I know. And now..." She smiled sweetly, hoping she wasn't laying it on too thick. "If you'd consider—just for this weekend's performances—taking the part? I'm sure you could learn the lines."

"I really can't stay in town that long."

"It would be a terrible imposition. You probably have all sorts of business meetings and social engagements planned, and I certainly wouldn't want to interfere with that." Her chin wobbled ever so slightly. Her drama teacher would have been impressed, not that Jennifer wasn't truly concerned about the future of Moraine. "Of course, if we can't make the payments we'll lose everything we've tried so hard to build. There'll be no more restoration projects, no more town."

As though on cue, Bonbon whined pathetically. She'd have to give him an extra bone for dinner.

Grady cleared his throat. "Look, I don't really have the time. Can't you call the casting office again?"

"I don't think it would do any good. At least not for this weekend, and weekends are the only time we put on the show. We'd never get someone up here in time." Hating herself for being so deceitful, she lightly touched his arm. She didn't usually flirt with men, most especially one whose gaze too often loitered on the rise and fall of her breasts. But the situation called for extraordinary measures. "And you would be good in the part. The audience would love you and—" she paused for effect "—I'd be particularly grateful."

She knew he was tempted, both by her and the fact that most people had a bit of "ham" in them. The dream of being a star was nearly universal, as she well knew. But the way his eyes narrowed with rejection, she also realized he was working up to refusing the offer. She would have to play her money card.

"You know, Grady, your investors would want you to do everything in your power to help us generate enough income to pay off the town's mortgages. It'd be a great sacrifice on your part to help us out this way, but I'm sure they'd be pleased." Her performance was very good.

Bonbon left her side and parked himself right in front of Grady. He looked up with doleful brown eyes.

"Are you sure there isn't some guy inside the fur rug?" Grady asked. He gave the dog a half-hearted pat.

"He doesn't always take to strangers so easily." Only those with ebony eyes that crinkle at the corners when he smiles, and dark hair that rakishly drapes across one brow.

"Lucky me. Maybe he wants another tie to chew on."

"Or maybe he's asking for forgiveness."

His dark gaze skimmed her from head to toe, sneaking under her skin, chafing and disturbing and nibbling at a barrier she'd long ago erected.

Her acting job was too effective, she realized. He was taking her flirtation quite seriously. Worse, she'd gotten herself so far into the part that she believed the attraction, too. She could feel the little catch in her throat, her breathlessness and the way the fabric of her dress seemed to be pulling tautly against her breasts. She hadn't meant to believe her own theatrics.

She hadn't intended to want him to stay for reasons that had nothing to do with paying off a mortgage.

"You said there's a rehearsal tonight?" he asked.

"At seven." Her voice cracked.

"Guess I could give it a try. If I'm not any good, at least you haven't lost anything."

"You'll be wonderful," she whispered.

Grady shifted his feet uncomfortably and eyed both the dog and the raccoon. Something strange was going on here. Jennifer Sweetham had managed to tame him as easily as she controlled her menagerie.

"I can probably put my time to good use if I hang around a couple of days," he said, rationalizing his decision to stay in Moraine. There'd been some very interesting and persistent inquiries about the mortgages on Moraine buildings; anonymous people fronted by a none-too-ethical attorney were offering an exceptionally large amount of money to buy up the overdue notes. It had made Grady curious enough that he'd wanted to investigate the situation for himself.

Glancing back at Jennifer he found her gazing at him, her lips parted slightly, the sunlight gilding her in a warm glow that begged for his touch, and he knew the investors were far from his mind. He had a much more compelling reason to want to stay in Moraine.

He'd never known eyes to be so persuasive. Their color made him think of cloudless skies and clear mountain lakes and long, lazy afternoons making love. He wondered if the blue would deepen when filled with passion, and hoped he'd have a chance to find out. A worthy ambition for a weekend in Moraine, he concluded.

He wasn't the kind of guy who impulsively changed his plans. He always carried one of those time management calendars in his coat pocket. Meetings were precisely noted in their appropriate place, deadlines marked in red, and social engagements in green. He'd led a rather ordered life. Until now. Until he'd been tempted by Jennifer Sweetham and the chance to stand behind the footlights again.

Mentally he put a big *X* through his weekend calendar pages. Now he could spend his time getting to know Jennifer. He imagined combing his fingers through her tumble of curls, testing the weight and texture of her hair, learning its scent. He'd find that sensitive spot just below her ear, explore there awhile and then move on to other delectable tastes and flavors she was sure to offer.

While Grady considered a whole range of pleasurable activities he intended to enjoy at the earliest opportunity, they turned and strolled together away from the house. Bonbon stretched, then inserted himself between them.

"Does your dog go everywhere you go?" he asked.

"Not always, but he loves to walk in the woods." She looked at him curiously. "Don't you like dogs?"

He shrugged. "I've never owned one."

"Then you're a cat lover."

"Nope." *I prefer to concentrate on gorgeous women, women like you.*

"Birds? Fish?"

"I had a boa constrictor when I was a teenager." *Over the rather hysterical objections of his mother.*

"A snake!" Jennifer cried.

He liked the way her eyes widened with fright, though since she'd been so cordial with the lizard he was surprised. "They're nice, quiet pets. They don't eat much and they can be quite affectionate."

"You've got to be kidding. Snakes and spiders give me the creeps."

"I also found a snake could be quite handy for all sorts of reasons. I used to get quite a reaction from the girls when they discovered my boa in the back seat of the car. Particularly on dark nights."

"Good grief," she laughed. "You are a villain."

"Not at all." Under the guise of reassuring Jennifer, he took her hand. His thumb rasped expertly along the delicate length of her fingers, heating her flesh beneath his. He stroked slowly, pleased when he felt her tremble. His seductive efforts had brought a response. The lady wasn't quite as prim as her costume suggested. "The whole idea was to show the girls what a hero I was. Just wait. If we come across a snake, I'll do my Superman imitation to save you."

"I should point out, Grady, we have rattlers in this part of the country. They're not exactly noted for their affectionate nature."

"In that case," he said smoothly, "you can sic Bonbon on it."

Lifting her hand, he pressed his lips to the soft spot between her thumb and finger, tasting her sweetness for just a moment before she pulled away from his grasp.

Visibly shaken, she walked ahead of him up the path.

The sunny slopes of the hills were dotted with oak trees, the ground covered with grass already turning summer brown. Myriad wildflowers in purple, yellow and white accented the rolling terrain while random outcroppings of granite looked like chess pieces discarded by a giant hand.

Pine trees marched down the slopes to meet the oaks, rich green contrasting with the dusty leaves on the sprawling giants. A redtail hawk hovered in an updraft, spying the ground for his dinner.

Grady could feel the stress of city living draining away, replaced by a different kind of tension brought on by the sexy woman walking near him. He slanted her a look, wondering why he found Jennifer Sweetham so provocative.

"Tell me," he asked, "do the residents of Moraine always dress in period costume?"

"Only in the summer for the tourist season. The rest of the time we're really quite normal."

Somehow he doubted that. Jennifer, at least, was far too special to be considered simply ordinary. Her uniqueness had an odd effect on his equilibrium. The magical feeling he'd experienced onstage still seemed to be affecting him.

He plucked a tall blade of grass and tucked it in his mouth. He'd forgotten how sweet grass could taste but it wasn't nearly as flavorful as Jennifer herself. "What do you do the rest of the year?"

"You mean me, personally? Or the town?" Her skirt made little rustling noises as she walked, and the floral-scented breeze tugged at the loose strands of her hair.

Grady tilted his lips into his most seductive smile and was gratified when Jennifer couldn't hold his gaze. "You first . . . and then the town," he persisted, aware she was feeling the tension between them as much as he.

"I teach English and drama at Sonora High School. That's about a half hour away." Self-consciously Jennifer snipped a sprig of mistletoe from an overhanging branch. She was uncomfortable talking about herself and acutely aware of Grady's closeness. Her hand still tingled where he'd kissed her; breathing had become strangely labored, and she felt flushed as though she were suddenly running a temperature. Assuming she could even gather her scattered thoughts, she doubted Grady would be interested in the joys she experienced as a teacher. Someone who spent his days trading in millions of dollars wouldn't understand.

"As soon as school's out," she responded instead, "all of us in Moraine start wearing our costumes. The children love it. They feel a real sense of purpose and pride adding to the ambience of the town."

"They do a good job. Had me doing a double take when I first arrived. I thought I'd stepped into a time-travel machine."

"There've been times when I wished I could do just that." Her voice carried a wistful note.

"You're not happy living in the twentieth century?"

She tossed aside the mistletoe. Bonbon, thinking he'd been invited to play a game of fetch, lumbered after it. His sudden movement startled a white-crowned sparrow from its perch, and a flock of blackbirds took to the air in frightened response.

"I'm very happy in Moraine," she said. "It's home. I wouldn't want anything to change."

"Time marches on. Progress."

"I suppose. But I'd hate to lose what's good about Moraine just in the name of progress. It wouldn't be a fair exchange." She would never again risk trading her friends and the view of forested mountains for urban excitement. That kind of life simply wasn't right for her.

"Even if the change would mean a lot more money for you and your friends?"

She paused and Grady watched as her lovely blue eyes narrowed. "I've never been very interested in money, Grady. It doesn't mean a thing without love and family. I think you'll find most of the people here feel the same way."

He wondered. In his experience, money was a temptation few people could resist. His father and Murdock Investments had based their entire existence on that premise. And whoever was trying to buy up the mortgages must surely have something big on their minds. Premium prices weren't offered without the hope of a hefty bottom line.

Trying to read Grady's thoughts, Jennifer studied the latest Moraine Theater cast member. Everything about him, from the expensive cut of his shirt to his polished shoes, spoke of wealth—and power.

Including the power to tear apart her hopes and dreams.

It didn't matter that Grady Murdock had a low, rumbling voice that seemed to play along her spine every time he spoke. It meant nothing that his smile could hold her mesmerized for a couple of heartbeats at a time. Or that his long, tapered fingers were both strong and gentle at once. The only thing that really mattered was Moraine. The one safe constant in her life. No way would she let him get his hands on her town. Whatever it took...

They reached the end of the track and circled back toward the house.

"Is there anyplace in town where I can get dinner?" Grady asked. "I hate the thought of getting back out on the highway again."

"The saloon serves meals. Nothing fancy."

"That's okay. I'll give it a try."

Good lord! Jake usually stopped in at the saloon for a quick beer on his way home from work. All that Jennifer needed was for Jake to start blabbing about his villain's role in the play and she'd be found out. She hadn't had a chance to tell anyone except Nyla what she was up to.

Lies always got a person into trouble. "Why don't you come back to our house for supper? It'd be no problem for Nyla to set an extra place."

"I don't want to put you out."

"You won't." She smiled weakly. She was definitely in over her head, and the charade had only just begun.

Ushering Grady in through the seldom-used front door of the house, Jennifer was struck by a new feeling of intimacy between them. He dominated the small room, bigger than life and many times more impressive. He took her breath away. His presence made her feel extraordinarily feminine and vulnerable. The sensation had been hard enough to manage with wide-open spaces around her. Now the feeling pressed against her in wave after wave of sensuous motion that made her dizzy with thoughts she didn't want to acknowledge.

"Just have a chair," she said, forcing the breath through her lungs, "and I'll—"

The swinging door between the kitchen and dining room swung open. "Do we have company?" Aunt Nyla asked. She bustled into the room, wiping her hands on her apron, her smile filled with friendliness.

"I'd like you to meet Grady Murdock, Aunt Nyla. He's the man who is going to fill in as Pierre. I told you about him earlier." She hoped Nyla would play along. "I've invited him to dinner."

Surprised, Nyla studied Grady over the top of her glasses. "Are you married, young man?"

"Nyla!"

Grady's lips curled in amusement. "No, ma'am. But if you're proposing, I'm definitely flattered."

Jennifer stifled a very unladylike word. "Please excuse my aunt. She sometimes forgets her manners."

"I do no such thing! Now you come on in the dining room, Mr. Murdock—"

"Grady, please," he corrected.

"And set yourself. I was just about to serve supper."

"We'll eat in the kitchen, Nyla. Just like we always do."

"Nonsense. Not when we've got company. You show the nice young man where to sit and I'll be back in a minute."

Jennifer gave Grady a hopeless look and followed her aunt into the kitchen.

"What on earth do you think you're doing?" Jennifer fumed.

"He is good-looking, isn't he?" Grinning smugly, Nyla pulled a roast out of the oven.

"What does that have to do with anything? He's the man who could foreclose on your house!"

"Then I guess you ought to be nice to the man 'cause I plan to stay right here until my ol' bones give out." Nyla filled two plates with sliced beef, mashed potatoes and vegetables she'd raised in her own garden. "Now you tell him there are plenty of seconds if this doesn't fill him up."

"You tell him. You're going to be right here." She had to accept the plates Nyla handed her or they would have dropped to the floor.

"Sorry." Nyla untied her apron. "I promised Millie I'd come visit awhile before rehearsal. Haven't seen her for ages."

"Did that happen since you put the roast in the oven?" Jennifer was incredulous. "You can't leave me alone with the man." *He's too damned attractive to be left alone with any woman.*

"Of course I can."

"But Danny will be here, won't he?" she asked suspiciously. *Her aunt was plotting against her.*

"I promised the boy he'd get to play with little Jason, Millie's grandson."

"Jason's only a baby."

"Danny likes babies." She leveled a knowing look at her niece. "He would really enjoy having a little brother or sister."

Jennifer sputtered. "Brother or—" It was hopeless. She knew that determined glint in her aunt's eye. She was going to have to pull this one off on her own.

And her aunt's matchmaking wasn't a part of the plan.

She pushed her way through the swinging door. "Dinner's ready." Placing the plates at the opposite ends of the scarred cherry wood table, she pulled out her chair. Before she could sit down Grady was there to help her, his breath a seductive whisper on her face as he bent near. Why did he have to be such a gentleman? "Sorry, but I guess it's only the two of us for dinner."

"I don't mind. I just don't want to be any trouble."

The only problem was the way Jennifer's heart kept beating in double-time whenever Grady came close. She wished he'd stop looking at her as if she were the main course. "Please. Enjoy your meal." It'd be even better if he took his dinner out onto the porch. Or maybe back to San Francisco. She'd be happy to give him a doggy bag.

He'd just taken his seat at the far end of the table when Nyla scurried into the room again. "I forgot something." She struck a match and lit the two candles in pewter holders. "There. That's better."

"Nyla, it's still broad daylight outside. We don't need candles." What was the woman trying to do?

Nyla, whose smile looked downright devious, puffed out the match. "You two have a good supper. And don't worry about the dishes. I'll take care of them when I get home." She hurried back into the kitchen.

Sighing, Jennifer said, "I'm really sorry. I don't know what has gotten into my aunt. She's not usually quite so—"

"She's charming. No need to apologize." He cut a bite of meat, forked it into his mouth and chewed slowly. He had the oddest feeling he was somehow out of time and place, the same sensation he'd had on Main Street. He was tempted to check the Rolex on his wrist to see what year it was and discarded the idea as being foolish. He was decidedly a twentieth century man. "Nyla's also one hell of a good cook. The only thing I can think to add to this meal is a bottle of wine—"

"Shh." Jennifer grimaced. "She's probably listening at the door. If she hears you she'll have us both tipsy before we get out of here."

Grady's laughter bounced around the walls, pinging deliciously against Jennifer's heart. Villains had no right to be quite so handsome and mesmerizing.

Chapter Three

Perched precariously on top of a ladder, Jennifer called to the cast member who played the role of the hero, Jack.

"Larry, can you help me with these overhead lights?"

"Sure, Jenny, I'll be right there." He climbed up the opposite side of the ladder to hold the light in place while she tightened the bolt.

"There. I got it." She let out a sigh. After her dinner with Grady she was a nervous wreck. Now she had to face the rehearsal. The first with Grady Murdock.

"Just as well Jake was working down in the valley today," Larry said.

"His wife tells me he won't be back until late. Maybe not even tomorrow morning." Jennifer hoped that would be the case. Things would be a real mess if Jake happened to show up and find Grady playing his part.

She and Larry climbed back down the ladder, and he placed it to the back of the nearly empty stage. Tonight they'd only be using a few metal chairs for props.

When Larry threw the switch for the lights, the stage was bathed in a harsh glow.

"Now listen up, people," Jennifer said to the cast.

Nyla, looking smug, played the role of the heroine's mother. She stood stage left talking to Marty VanPelten, the local banker cast as Candice's drunkard father.

"The idea," she explained, "is to act like Grady is simply doing us a favor for the weekend by taking the part of Pierre. We won't say anything about the mortgages."

"Does he know that we know he represents Sierra Syndications?" Marty asked. A troubled expression crossed his narrow face.

"He told me who he is, so he'll assume I've told you. It won't matter as long as he's having a good time doing the melodrama. He'll stay the weekend and then we'll have a chance to get him on our side."

"I hope he can act," Larry said, running his fingers through his blond hair. Onstage or off, Larry Brevik suited the soft-spoken role of hero. "I'd hate for us to lay an egg on opening night."

"He'll do fine," Jennifer assured them. Based on her own reactions, Grady could muff every one of his lines and the ladies in the audience would still come close to swooning.

Nervous, she shrugged off her shawl and draped it over a chair.

When she looked up, her heart tapped a staccato beat.

Grady stood in the doorway, now wearing a windbreaker over his cotton shirt. How could she have forgotten in only an hour how wickedly attractive he was? His shoulders were broader than she remembered, and his torso tapered to lean hips above his long legs. His shirt tugged snugly across his chest. She had an urge to straighten his collar and run her hands around the back of his neck where his dark hair just brushed the top of his jacket. It was all she could do to recall the danger he represented to the town instead of focusing on needs she'd long ago repressed.

Her mouth gone dry, she futilely licked her lips.

Deliberately, she forced a calmness she didn't feel and introduced Grady to the rest of the cast.

"We'll just run through Pierre's scenes," she said, handing Grady a dog-eared script. "That'll give you a feel for what we're doing."

"You're going to have to help me out a lot," Grady insisted. "I really haven't done this sort of thing since high school."

"You'll be great. With this kind of play all you have to do is overact and the audience will think it's wonderful fun."

Larry stepped forward. "Wait till you hear the boos and hisses. You'll get a kick out of it."

"While you get all of the applause?" Grady asked dryly, raising an eyebrow.

"Us hero types deserve all the applause we can get."

With an appreciative chuckle, Marty gave the younger man a slap on the back.

Jennifer sorted out the cast and put them to work.

With only a little encouragement, Grady began to relax and be as campy as the rest of them.

While she directed the action, another part of her brain studied Grady with considerable interest. He learned his lines so quickly she wondered if he had a photographic memory.

To her delight, he was also quick to laugh, even when he made a mistake. When his tongue got twisted around *my precocious pretty* for the third time, he said, "Maybe you ought to call the casting office one more time." His dark eyes glistened with self-amusement, and then he tried the line again with complete success.

The harsh overhead lights emphasized the rugged shape of his jaw and cast shadows beneath his cheek bones. Grady's nose had a slight bend she hadn't noticed before, as though it had been broken. It gave him an earthy, man-of-action quality in contrast to the precision-pressed image he'd presented the first time she'd seen him.

She felt herself slipping from lustful attraction into admiration for Grady. Not a good idea. Not with so much at stake, both personally and for the town.

"Let's do the scene where the villain comes to claim his bride," Jennifer announced. "Page forty-six, I think."

Everyone ruffled through their scripts and Jennifer glanced at her part. Knowing there was no way to avoid this particular scene, she drew a shaky breath.

Grady entered from stage right and swept his imaginary cloak aside.

"Your father cannot pay the mortgage, sweet Candice," he said as villainous Pierre. His fingers twirled the tip of his mustache. "The house is mine . . . and all that is in it."

"No! No!" Jennifer cried, her hand covering her heart. "You cannot be so cruel. It is cold and wintry. The snow is deep on the ground." Her hand fluttered in the general direction of outside. "If you send us out into the night, we shall all perish."

Her lines were delightfully predictable, and she played off Grady's thoroughly evil villain. Whether he knew it or not, he was a natural actor with a marvelous flair for the dramatic. Their give-and-take was good. She could sense it in the way the other characters responded. An audience would love it. And Grady.

She feigned a faint and Pierre caught her in his arms.

"Ah, you cannot escape your fate, dear heart," he said. "To protect your family, you will be my wife."

She knew what was coming. In every melodrama the villain manages to kiss the heroine once.

But nothing had prepared Jennifer for the shock of Grady's mouth on hers for the first time. His lips were gentle, his touch a mastery of subtle seduction, the softness of his mustache a velvet brush. The quick

path of his tongue across her lower lip sent a shivery
need through her entire body, turning her liquid in an
effortless moment. If he hadn't been holding her, she
was sure she would have sunk to the floor.

Her heart hammered in her chest. Instinctively she
clung to the lapels of his jacket. She'd fallen out of
character. The only role she felt was that of Jennifer,
her mouth hungry for Grady, her body crying out to
be pulled closer by his muscular arms. With an urgency she'd never before experienced, she opened to
the gentle penetration of his tongue. He tasted as fresh
as a mountain spring. She eagerly drank in his flavor.

He intensified the kiss, probing, exploring, demanding a response that she gave in equal measure.
He claimed her lips, her mouth, her very soul and
changed her in ways she had never before understood. Conquered, she offered no resistance. The
hunger she felt was too deep to conceal.

The rest of world faded away like meaningless
props on an empty stage. The warmth of his arms
branded her indelibly through the cotton of her dress.
His lips seared their shape and texture into her memory. Barely repressing a moan, she arched into the nest
of his hips and felt honeyed moisture form between
her thighs.

In response to her surrender, his hand slid slowly
down her back, traveling the curve of her hips until it
rested on her buttocks, pinning her with ease against
his lean, hard body. He was muscle and sinew,
strength and power. She felt his coiled passion building within him, colliding with her own.

Seconds or minutes passed. She couldn't be sure, held as she was in the still frame of his embrace.

Finally he broke the kiss.

Blinking under the bright lights, Jennifer struggled to bring her senses back to reality. It was a kiss in a play. No more. She was an actor and, for tonight, so was he. In real life they were more adversaries than lovers. But if the kiss had meant nothing, why was she still spinning out of control?

Could he have felt the explosive power, too?

Her lines. She had the next line. Her memory nearly failed her, she felt so disoriented.

"No! Never shall I be your wife for I love another," she managed to say in a voice that sounded strangely distant and unfamiliar. Following the stage directions, she turned to exit and blindly fell over a chair, landing on the floor with a bone-jarring jolt.

The entire cast raced to her aid, friendly hands helping her to a sitting position. She was breathless and shaken but uninjured. Dammit, of all the times to do something stupid. She didn't want Grady or anybody else to think his kiss had been the cause of her misstep. That wasn't the case...at least not the sole reason.

"Are you all right, Jen?" Grady knelt beside her.

"I'm fine. Really. I forgot the chair was there."

"Ooo-eee! If a man like Grady kissed me like that, I'd forget my own name." Nyla's happy laughter echoed around the vacant stage and was repeated by the rest of the cast.

Jennifer grimaced. "The chair shouldn't have been—I just lost my concentration for a moment."

"Looked to me like you an' Grady were concentrating real good," Marty laughed.

"That's not why—" What was the use in denying what had happened, Jennifer thought with resignation. It only made matters worse. And their laughter louder.

"Hey, I thought the hero was supposed to get the girl in this show," Larry complained good-naturedly. "Thought sure it was a clause in my union contract."

"Don't count on it, Larry." Grady's eyes gleamed with wicked laughter.

Chagrined, she allowed Grady to help her up. The heat of his hand at her elbow sent a surge of warmth to fill a spot near her heart, a place she hadn't even realized was empty. His grip tightened slightly, speaking volumes about the barely controlled passion they'd nearly unleashed.

An image flashed through her mind, their bodies melded together, their sweat-dampened flesh gilded by firelight, and she knew she didn't dare think about that...about the very thing Grady made her want more than anything else in the world—a shockingly quick end to her years of self-imposed celibacy.

Instead Jennifer insisted she was fine to continue the rehearsal and kept the cast working for another half hour. But she didn't suggest they repeat the kissing scene. Grady didn't need any coaching in that department, nor did she want to risk a repeat performance.

"It's ten o'clock, people," she announced, relieved the rehearsal was over. "Let's call it a night. Dress rehearsal tomorrow at seven and then we'll be ready for the performance."

Amid the good-nights, Marty sidled up beside her. The gray wisps of hair that he combed in a useless effort to cover his balding head had drooped to the side.

Giving her shoulders a squeeze, he whispered, "You're doing a great job keeping that young man in town. After that kiss it'd take a team of wild horses to get him to leave. Best job of acting I've ever seen, Jenny. Always knew you had star quality."

A knot formed in Jennifer's stomach. What she had experienced in Grady's arms had been no act. But if he ever found out she'd conspired to keep him in town, he would never believe it.

Grady joined them from across the stage. "How 'bout I drop in to see you first thing in the morning, Marty? I've got some business to discuss."

"Tomorrow? I, ah, don't know..."

"I'll come by at ten. That's when you open, right?"

Marty looked helplessly at Jennifer. All she could do was twist her mouth into an I-don't-know-what-else-you-can-do smile.

"Sure it can't wait till after Founder's Day?" Marty asked hopefully. "Got a lot to do gettin' ready for the big doings."

"Like lizard races."

"That's right. Darn exciting. Those little critters can really skedaddle."

"No doubt." Grady ran his fingers carelessly through his dark hair. "My business won't take long."

Marty's bushy eyebrows drew together. "If you insist. Big-city folks are always in such a rush," he mumbled as he headed out the stage door. "Seems to me things like mortgages could wait a day or two."

Grady turned to Jennifer. "I'd say you people operate with a different set of priorities than we have in the city."

"You're probably right," she conceded.

She reached for her shawl but Grady picked it up first. He slipped it gently around her shoulders. When he lifted her hair to adjust the shawl, his breath warmed her neck like a soft summer breeze. She remembered the sweet flavor of his mouth, and tightness constricted her throat. The impulsive desire to taste him again warred with her good sense.

She wanted, needed, Grady to stay in town until Founder's Day but couldn't allow him to disrupt the life she'd so carefully built for herself and her son.

"I'll walk you home," he said.

"It really isn't very far." But farther than she ought to allow him to come.

"It's right on my way." He circled his arm around her waist in a proprietary way that was both annoying and achingly pleasant at the same time. She knew she ought to find the courage or will to step away but failed in the effort.

The moon seemed brighter than usual, big and yellow and smiling. Shadows crisscrossed the ground almost as crisply as midday. The night air, tinged with the scent of pine, cooled Jennifer's heated flesh but did little to calm the turmoil building within her. A growing sense of Grady's nearness skittered along her spine and burrowed itself low in her body.

Grady drew her closer. "I suppose you have to get home to your son."

"He's staying with friends just a few houses away. He usually does when I have a late rehearsal or a performance."

"Then there's no rush. We can enjoy the evening."

"But I really do have to get home," she insisted with as much authority as she could muster. "I have a million things yet to do for Founder's Day."

"Big doings."

"Yes." Her answer was little more than a weak whisper.

"Hmm." He pulled her off the path into the deep shadows of a pine. "I was hoping we'd have a chance to rehearse that kiss one more time. I'm not sure I got it quite right."

"You did fine. Quite—" she swallowed hard "—professionally."

He lifted her chin and rasped his thumb along her lower lip. The sensation of flesh moving on sensitive flesh skated along her nerve endings.

Her heart raced, filling her body with a rhythmic beat. "I don't think we should..."

The warmth of his hand cupped her cheek and she fought the urge to rest her face against the pillows of his palm. Slowly he lowered his mouth toward hers.

Cords of opposing panic and need looped themselves through her stomach and knotted there.

"Thinking's not always a good idea, Jenny. Following your instincts can be much more exciting."

Grady brushed her lips with his, knowing Jennifer's instincts were as passionate as his. He'd felt that onstage. All she needed was a little nurturing, just good old-fashioned seduction.

He drew her lower lip between his teeth, suckling and nibbling gently. She trembled. A low-throated groan whispered up her throat. Smiling to himself, he let his tongue circle her lips, soothing the sensitive flesh. God she tasted good. So sweet. And hot. Hotter than she knew.

Jennifer braced her hands on his broad chest, tempted to give in to the madness of Grady Murdock, to the frantic sensory signals that sparked from each millimeter of flesh he touched. Her body keened for his. Every nerve shimmered in the anticipation of what they would be together, what he would do with her and she to him. Irrationally she craved his heat, wanted to lick it off, bask in it without fear of being burned.

But that wasn't possible, she warned herself.

With a willpower she hadn't imagined possible, she slipped away from his embrace and out of the shadows onto the moonlit path.

He caught her hand before she could entirely escape.

"Grady. I don't want this." His grip was a tender vise, holding Jennifer against her will.

"There's something happening between us, Jenny. I felt it onstage and I think you did, too. Don't say no till we've explored it a bit."

"It's just hormones . . . the mountain air."

"It might be worth pursuing. I'm here for the weekend. . . ."

His reference to only the next few days jolted her. She wouldn't give in to the temptation of Grady Murdock. A single weekend wouldn't be worth the pain. "Please don't do this to me."

Tensing, he studied her with dark, curious eyes. "Maybe I read you wrong earlier. Is there already a man in your life?" His thumb rasped along her knuckles.

"Man?"

"You know. A hero type. Maybe tall and blond."

"It's nothing like that." They'd both bought her flirtatious act. Nyla's antics at dinner hadn't helped. Only Jennifer would suffer the consequences.

"Then it seems to me the field is open. I'm available. So are you. Think of it as welcoming a stranger to town."

Unwilling to pay the emotional price, she pulled her hand from his. "I'm a mountain girl, Grady. I like lizard races and chili bake-offs. You can think of me as a country bumpkin if you'd like, but that's who I am. If I misled you, I'm sorry. I'm not into weekend flings, and I don't fit in with guys from the city with laptop computers."

"I haven't turned my computer on all day," he said wryly.

"You know what I mean."

He jammed his hands in his pockets. "Maybe if the right guy came along you'd change your mind." He wasn't used to rejection and she sure had seemed interested onstage. Here in the moonlight, too. She was doing a good job of ignoring what he knew to be true.

For a heartbeat she hesitated. "I don't think so."

Grady heard her pause and viewed it as a challenge. He'd had smaller windows of opportunity in his life and had managed to close the deal. All it took was the right approach.

As he watched her figure retreat up the path, he softly warned, "Don't think for a minute that's the end of our discussion, Jennifer Sweetham."

Chapter Four

An angry squawk woke Grady.

A bird? In his condo?

Groggy, Grady concluded he must have fallen asleep with the window open and a demented pigeon with a sore throat had made its way into his home.

He pried one eye open. Unless someone had redecorated his condo with knotty-pine paneling, he was definitely not in his own bed.

He rolled his head to the side and found himself staring at the beady eye of a Steller's jay who sat on his windowsill. The bird fluffed his bright blue feathers nonchalantly, as though preening for Grady's approval. Either the jay was a very cheeky fellow or thought he owned the whole forest.

Another half-wild creature tamed by the local heroine?

A rush of memory, of Jennifer and the kiss they'd shared onstage, brought Grady fully awake. She'd definitely gotten under his skin…and into his dreams.

A serious distraction for a man who had business on his mind and a banker to visit.

During the night, thoughts of her soft lips, the thick silkiness of her hair, the way her body had molded against his, had kept him staring into the darkness for hours. Even now, as he sat up and swung his legs over the side of the bed, her special scent still seemed to hover nearby making his libido rev up a notch or two.

He wanted her. Right now. In his arms. In his bed. More than any woman he could ever remember wanting before. But she was certainly not the kind of gal he'd been looking for. He almost laughed at the thought of her settling into his penthouse condo. Unless, of course, she was willing to turn a whole lot of messy pigeons into pets.

He'd better listen to his head, he decided, and not to certain other parts of his anatomy that lacked the ability to make rational decisions.

The jay hopped brazenly onto the chest of drawers. He rooted among the coins Grady had emptied from his pockets when he undressed for bed.

"Get outta there," Grady grumbled.

With an angry squawk, the bird hopped back to the windowsill. Grady caught a glimpse of a silver coin in the jay's beak and lunged for the bird.

Effortlessly the bird took flight, leaving Grady on his knees shouting furiously, "Bring me back my dollar, you—" He pounded his fist on the sill.

Boldly the bird stared back at him from a pine branch just out of reach. Son of a—

"Here birdie, birdie," Grady crooned, taking a softer approach. He straddled the windowsill, one leg dangling in the air, his eye on the coin in the bird's mouth. "That's a nice birdie. Bring ol' Grady back the dollar and I'll give you a cracker. Birdie want a cracker?"

He felt like an idiot talking to the stupid bird. He only wished he had a butterfly net. Then he could capture the bird without doing any permanent damage to the latest Moraine thief. If that jay was Jennifer's feathered friend, he wouldn't want to harm a single, precious tail feather.

But desperate measures were called for when his lucky dollar was at stake. It was the only gift Grady's father had personally given him. He could still remember his father placing the hand-warmed dollar in his palm, a reward for a seven-year-old's first home run. An event his dad had missed. Like all the other special moments in his young life. And the last silver dollar Grady had ever received.

The next time he hit a home run, Grady hadn't bothered to tell his old man.

Grady leaned out the cabin window a little farther. If he could just reach the branch, maybe he could jiggle it and dislodge the bird, making him drop—

The bird flapped its wings...and flew right at Grady.

"No-o-o-o..."

Unbalanced, he teetered on the windowsill, then crashed into the low-growing bushes and onto the rocky ground.

With his first breath he let out a string of curses that would have done a sailor proud.

Unconcerned, the jay swept down toward the cottage roof and then vanished out of sight in the direction of Jennifer's house, the silver dollar still glinting in his beak.

"It figures." Jennifer was like Fagan in *Oliver Twist,* except instead of teaching London urchins to pick pockets, she managed to train her wild creatures to snatch stuff right out of his hands.

He struggled up and trudged around to the front of the cabin to let himself back in. Rocks dug into his bare feet. He itched from head to toe with prickly pine needles and could only hope he hadn't fallen into any poison oak.

Back in the cabin he showered and shaved, his image in the mirror often replaced with Jennifer's heart-shaped face. More than once he had to blink away the sight of her blue eyes staring back at him. He barely avoided taking a second, and very cold, shower.

His mood still unsettled when he'd finished dressing, he headed toward the bank. He didn't like the feel of his empty trouser pocket. Any other coin wouldn't have mattered. He'd had that silver dollar a long time. Out of long habit, he always gave it a quick little rub before he signed his name on the dotted line for any risky investment. Not that he really believed it made any difference, he assured himself.

Even so, Jennifer had damn well better know where that bird had taken his lucky piece.

Outside the bank he shifted his shoulders and eased the tension from his neck. Emotion and business didn't mix. Overdue as the town was on the mortgage payments, he was sure he could convince Marty VanPelten to tell him what was going on in Moraine.

He stepped inside. The scent of ink pads and old money enveloped him. The teller's window with its arched ironwork was straight out of the past. The oak countertop was etched with years of hard use. He could almost see a line of miners with little pouches in their hands waiting to have their gold weighed. Eerie.

Marty sat at a wooden desk at the back of the small bank. Wearing a dark vest over a stiff-collared shirt, and a string tie, he looked very much in character as the local banker. The older man glanced up and peered at Grady across the top of half glasses.

"Well, now, you're a prompt man." Marty closed the cover on a heavy accounting ledger. "I like that in a man. Yes, sir. Like that a whole lot." He extended his bony hand to Grady. An ink stain smudged his middle finger.

"Interesting bank you have here, Marty."

"Been in the family for better'n a hundred years." He jerked his head toward a row of portraits, each one a balding man with Marty's narrow-set eyes. "My boy will be the next VanPelten to run the place. Wally's studying at Harvard now."

Grady suspected a Harvard grad might well want to make changes in the anachronism called Moraine Bank, and he wondered how Marty would feel about that.

"I'm sure you're very proud of him," Grady said smoothly, taking a seat in the leather chair across from Marty.

"Crackerjack boy, that son of mine. Smart as a whip." Beaming with fatherly pride, he turned a framed photograph on his desk so Grady could see the lanky, next-generation VanPelten banker. The family resemblance was apparent, particularly around the eyes.

Grady made an appropriately noncommittal comment. "As you know, Marty, Sierra Syndications is carrying the mortgages on most of the buildings in town and we've been concerned about—"

"No need for you and your investors to get worried. No reason at all." Marty tapped his fingertip on top of the ledger. "We've got the numbers all figured out. We'll be up-to-date with our payments faster than you can say Tuolumne County."

"That wasn't precisely our concern. From our original research we're confident the town will eventually be able to cover the debt." Grady stretched out his legs and hooked one ankle over the other. "We've been wondering if there were some plans for further development, something that might have attracted a lot of interest."

A suspicious scowl darkened Marty's narrow face. "Development?"

"A big influx of money maybe? A large investment group trying to set up an expansion program?"

"You know, Grady, when you start talkin' development, that makes me a sight nervous. Besides, most of our historic buildings are listed in the registry now. Can't mess around with them.''

''Most people are aware of that, but there are ways to get around the rules, if you know the right people. This is prime recreational country, particularly for the people who live in the San Francisco area and are looking for a weekend escape.''

Marty's expression looked pained. ''Are you planning to turn this into an amusement park?''

Grady chuckled and plucked a piece of lint from his gray slacks. ''I'm not, but there've been some inquiries that led me to believe a pretty high-powered group might have some plans we don't know about. I thought, as the local banker, you might have heard some rumors.''

Shaking his head and nervously shifting in his chair, Marty said, ''No one around here would want to turn Moraine into some kind of a circus. We like things just as they are. You stick around for a couple of days and you'll see what I mean.''

Grady was about to agree, thinking he intended to learn more about both the town and its heroine, when a jeans-clad man burst into the bank. Compactly built with broad shoulders, his muscular arms looked too long for his body.

''Hey, Marty, I've got time to fix the leak in your roof now, if it's okay.''

''Right, Jake.'' Marty bustled up and hurried toward the workman. ''You go on ahead with whatever you have to do.''

Jake spotted Grady sitting by the desk. Ignoring Marty, he strode past the swinging gate and shook Grady's hand.

"Always glad to see strangers in town," Jake said. From his hip pocket he pulled out a piece of paper. "Carry these flyers around for our melodrama and give 'em out every chance I get." He pointed to the picture above the typed information. "That's me. The evil villain. If you're in town tomorrow, you won't want to miss our show."

Marty tried to snatch away the yellow flyer.

Slowly Grady stood, not relinquishing the announcement for Moraine Theater. "You're the villain?" His gaze traveled up and down the very healthy-looking Jake, noting the absence of a cast or any other indication he'd been injured recently.

"You bet I am." Jake wiggled his dark eyebrows and smiled fiendishly.

"You haven't had a broken leg lately?" Grady asked.

"Gosh, no. Healthy as an ox. That's me."

Marty mumbled something about getting on with the roofing job and shoved at Jake's bulk to get him out of the bank.

With an affable "So long. Don't forget the melodrama," Jake pushed out through the door.

Grady's blood pressure rose by several degrees.

Somebody had been trying to scam him, Grady thought, and he knew just who was probably at the bottom of it. Even so, the surge of anger that knotted his stomach startled him with its intensity. It was raw and burning, a repeat of the pain he'd felt when he'd caught the woman he was planning to marry in a blatant lie.

Jennifer had conned him into staying in town by saying he was a good actor. She could turn the charm on and off so easily.

He'd been a fool. Tripped up by a bird and a woman all within twenty-four hours.

He'd sworn he wouldn't fall into that trap again. Ever.

He made a conscious effort to settle his shoulders and unclench hands that had balled into fists.

It would be no skin off his nose if he sold the mortgages to the highest bidder. He just had to make sure his investors got a good price.

"You do understand," Grady said to Marty, enunciating each word very carefully, "that with the payments in arrears it may be in the best interests of the investors to sell off the notes. We wouldn't be responsible for who purchased them or what their development plans might be."

Marty paled visibly. "We were hoping you would come around to our point of view."

"I don't think I'm interested in sticking around that long."

JENNIFER PULLED BACK her hair and held it in place with a ribbon that matched the patchwork pastels of her dress. She wasn't exactly pleased with the woman she saw in the mirror.

Damn, why had she lied to Grady?

She ran her fingers lightly across her lips. The memory of their kisses seemed to linger there, warm and seductive, inviting an encore, prickling at something basic and primal within her. Like the warmth of spring sunshine, he'd stirred dormant feelings she'd been ignoring for years.

Gazing at her reflection, she remembered another man whose kisses had tempted her. What a disastrous mistake. He'd been more interested in making his first million dollars than in making a commitment to her and the child they'd created together.

Forcefully she put the painful memory aside. Being honest with Grady was one thing, but she wouldn't let their relationship go further than that. She didn't want another high-powered executive in her life. She would never, ever risk subjecting Danny to such bruising rejection.

As though sensing her troubled mood, Bonbon rested his head in her lap and whined sympathetically.

"Come on, sweetheart, it's confession time." She consoled the dog with a scratch behind his ears. "And for heaven's sake, be nice to Grady. No more tienapping."

Before she left the house, she quickly straightened up the living room, putting away Danny's miniature cars in his make-believe garage made out of a cardboard carton. Smiling, she felt the familiar swell of love in her chest.

Outside she glanced anxiously at the cottage where Grady had stayed the night, but decided he'd probably already gone to see Marty at the bank. She hurried along the path to Main Street, Bonbon at her side.

She had nearly reached the end of the path when she saw Grady. In an instant she knew he'd learned of her deception. He was like a violent summer storm, dark and menacing and marching toward her with angry strides, so devastatingly compelling in his fury it took her breath away.

Grady ground to a stop in front of her. "I want my dollar back!" He spat out the words between tight lips.

She blinked. "I beg your pardon?" Those weren't the words she'd expected to hear. Her gaze slipped from his dark eyes to the sensuous shape of his mouth, as though she were trying to discern if her ears had failed her.

"Your damn bird came into my bedroom and snatched my silver dollar right off the dresser. I want it back."

"I don't know what you're talking about. I thought you'd been talking with Marty and had found out—"

"Oh, I've found out a lot this morning. Like you're a really good actress, on and offstage. Or else ol' Jake sure has quick-mending bones. Or maybe folks recover faster with a little mountain air."

A twinge of guilt made her stomach knot. "I was just coming to tell you—"

"Yeah, I bet. Just like I won the lottery."

"I really am sorry I lied to you, Grady. You have every right to be angry with me, but shouting doesn't help. I simply didn't know what else to do." She lifted her chin and straightened her spine, wishing she couldn't remember quite so clearly the sensation of his mouth on hers. "I said the first thing that came to mind. The whole town knew you had come here to foreclose and I—"

"Foreclose?" His dark eyebrows knitted into a solid line, villainously attractive.

"Of course. It's no secret your syndicate holds the mortgages on most of the buildings in town. We needed the money so we could do all the restoration and turn Moraine into—"

"We aren't going to foreclose. After my informative little chat with Jake, the villain, I'll leave foreclosure plans up to the new investors."

"You'd let a whole town be destroyed because you're mad at me?" She set her jaw into a grim line. No one had the right to be that petty no matter how physically attractive he might be. She would simply ignore the fact that Grady was broad-shouldered and a hundred eighty pounds of masculine intimidation. She wasn't going to notice the tantalizing brush of dark hair visible at the V of his sport shirt, or wonder what it would feel like to touch the crisp curls that no doubt furred his chest.

"It'll depend on what's best for the investors."

"Is that all you're worried about? Making the almighty dollar?"

"My dear Ms. Sweetham," he said. The lines around his lips drew taut, yet his mouth appeared just as seductive as ever. "We've had a very lucrative offer. One that's very difficult to turn down. I don't know for sure what they're up to, but it smells of a big development to me."

"You can't let that happen. Not here."

His dark eyes raked her angrily. "At this point, Ms. Sweetham, I don't much give a damn what happens to your town."

She leveled him an icy look. "We don't want any more development."

"And just what was it you wanted, Jennifer?" He eyed her speculatively, the insinuation in his tone like a sharp knife to her heart. "Are you just a tease, or was the local heroine ready to give up her virtue to save the town from foreclosure? Is that what your little act was all about?"

"Not a chance, Mr. Murdock. Dream on."

"How far would you be willing to go to keep your precious town just as it is? What's your price?"

She resisted the impulse to slap Grady's face. Acting childishly wouldn't solve anything. "I don't have a price, Mr. Murdock. Not one you could pay. The town council simply hoped we could get you to stick around long enough so we could show you a different kind of life, a different way to have fun and enjoyment. For the children. That's what Moraine is all about."

"It's always been about money and profit. It's strictly business, sweetheart. Bottom line."

Bonbon, agitated by the anger around him, pawed at Grady's leg and he shoved the animal away.

"That's all that matters to you, isn't it?" she accused. "Money. Stuffing your pockets with it." Men equated money with control, and she'd had enough of that in her life. So many other things were far more important.

"It's my job. I put together investment packages that make a profit. The Murdocks have been doing that for three generations. It's called capitalism, in case you've forgotten your high school economics lesson."

"I remember. All too well." And she recalled another man who thought money was the only thing that mattered. Grady was simply another villain she didn't need in her life.

Bonbon groveled at Grady's feet and swept his shaggy tail across the dirt path as though it was his job to keep the area neat.

Glancing at his Rolex, Grady said, "I've got time to do some checking around in Sonora and still make it back to San Francisco early enough to make a deal with the new investors. Then you can make your sweet offers to them."

"Please don't do that. At least wait till Monday. It's only fair to give the town a chance, and a few days won't matter to your profit margin, will they?" She only hoped that behind his devilish black eyes there was a reasonable man. "If you'd just stay through Founder's Day and see the first tourists. The kids are wonderful with them. It's so very special."

"No. I've had it with this town, and you." His angry gaze grated across her flesh, giving her a tight, painful thrill in spite of herself. "Just see to it I get my dollar back."

"Your dollar?" she asked acidly. Digging into the pocket in the folds of her dress, she drew out a paper dollar. "Of course, Mr. Murdock. A dollar saved is a dollar earned, right? I certainly wouldn't want the town of Moraine to cause you any financial hardship." With great dignity, she carefully placed the dollar in his shirt pocket. "Thanks so much for the dance, Mr. Murdock," she said sarcastically.

Reacting to Jennifer's gesture, Bonbon leapt eagerly to his feet. All bulk and little grace, he caught Grady off guard and nearly knocked him down.

With a curse, Grady regained his balance. "Keep that mutt away from me! And all the rest of your circus animals."

How could a woman who looked like an angel lie like the devil's own handmaiden? He didn't like a female who could sneak under his skin with a seductive smile and leave him sleepless half the night.

Jennifer Sweetham had turned him sour on innocence, he thought as he stormed up the path to pack his bags. From now on he was going to keep his feet solidly in the twentieth century.

He jammed his hands in his pockets. "Fool bird," he muttered.

JENNIFER STOOD rooted in place until the cottage door slammed behind Grady. Her body trembled with anger and she wanted to scream in frustration, though she wouldn't dream of letting Grady know just how upset she was.

Somewhere low in her stomach she felt another sensation, an aching sense of loss, a chance missed for some tremendous discovery that had escaped her all of her life. The closing door had cut her off from a vision she'd just barely glimpsed and could scarcely understand.

It wasn't as if anything had changed, she told herself. In fact, Grady had said he wasn't going to foreclose on the town, at least for the moment. There was a threat of some unknown development, but that seemed very distant and clouded.

Even the melodrama would go on as usual, with Jake playing the part of Pierre. With luck the ticket sales might be enough to cover the back mortgage payments. Moraine would be safe.

Turning her back to the cabin, she called Bonbon.

"Come on, fella. We aren't going to let anybody destroy our town." And no devilish rogue with captivating eyes and a ton of sex appeal was going to break her heart.

Chapter Five

"Hey, mister."

Suitcase in hand, Grady dragged his thoughts away from Jennifer and glanced down at the small boy beside him. Danny Sweetham looked at him with eyes just as blue and fully as beguiling as those of his mother.

"What do you want, Danny?"

"Have you seen my lizard?"

Grady looked up and down the dusty Main Street of town. The only person in sight was Jake propping a ladder against the overhanging roof outside the bank. The biting odor of hot roofing tar filled the air.

He shook his head. "Sorry, kid."

"Ralph's real big. He's gonna win the race."

"Ralph?"

"That's what I named him."

Of course. A perfectly good name for a lizard. Certainly as reasonable as Bonbon for a Behemoth and Zorro for a masked bandit. "But you lost him?"

"Yeah." Danny's chin wobbled. "I was showing my friends how fast he could run. He ran so fast he got away. Mom said I shouldn'a let him outta the box."

"Mothers sometimes know what's best." Even beautiful mothers who tease and flirt enough to drive a man crazy... then lied behind their honey-colored lashes. Still, that was no reason for her son to suffer.

He set his suitcase on the ground and cupped the boy's shoulder. "Which way did he go, tiger?"

"Under the porch." Danny pointed under the raised boardwalk. "Everybody left and Ralph's all alone...." Unshed tears glistened in the child's eyes.

"Guess you'll have to crawl around under there and see if you can find him."

Jake brushed past them with a bucket of hot roofing tar. "Don't forget the melodrama tomorrow. Great show." He agilely started up the ladder.

Danny blinked up at Grady, his lower lip quivering again. "I... don't wanna go under there."

"Why not?"

"There's goblins 'n' stuff. My friends told me."

"I don't think so, son." It wouldn't do Grady's slacks and monogrammed sport shirt any good if he went rooting around under the bank. But he guessed it would be worth the cleaning bill if he could help the kid find his pet. "How about we crawl under there together?"

The child hesitated, visibly weighing his fear against his desire to get his lizard back.

"Guess Ralph wouldn't wanta be left all alone with goblins," the boy finally said.

"You're very brave to understand that, Danny."

The child chewed on his lower lip and tried for a tentative smile.

There wasn't much room under the porch. Maybe eighteen inches. Powdery fine dirt, smelling dry and sterile, tickled Grady's nose and crept past the waistband of his trousers. Dusty spiderwebs crossed between the beams above his head. A few wisps brushed across his face.

He scooted along on his stomach thinking Danny had the advantage of size in such close quarters. Even so, he understood why a kid of six wouldn't want to face goblins that lurked almost everywhere in a young child's imagination.

Something wet and sloppy flicked across Grady's ear.

Startled, he rolled in the opposite direction.

"Geez, Bonbon, what the hell are you doing here?" The dog belly-crawled toward him, his tail sweeping the dirt into a cloud. Any minute now Jennifer would join the party. Then they'd have a high ol' time. The urge to throttle her still warred with the desire to kiss her again. Tough lady to forget.

"There he is!" Danny cried, spotting the lizard. The boy scuttled past Grady on all fours.

Bonbon followed suit.

Ralph had come to rest on one of the six-by-six posts supporting the boardwalk. Startled by Danny's cry and the threatening approach of the dog, the lizard dropped to the ground and set his legs into a furious effort at escape.

Danny charged after him.

Tail wagging, Bonbon elbowed his way after the boy.

Grady maneuvered to block Ralph's path.

The lizard faked left, like a wide receiver, and juked to the right toward the street.

On elbows and knees, Grady scrambled after the dog, the close confines beneath the boardwalk slowing his pace.

Grady, Danny, Bonbon and the lizard all popped out into the sunlight together. Then things began to happen so quickly Grady had only vague impressions.

Danny shouted, "I've got him!"

A deeper male voice cried, "The ladder! Watch out for the—"

Bonbon barked.

Grady scrambled to his feet. He shouted, "It's bad luck to—" In a futile effort, he lunged to hold Jake's ladder in place. It slipped from his grasp. At the same moment he linked his arm around Danny's waist to drag him safely away from the falling ladder and hot tar.

There was a lot of shouting. Tar sizzled onto the ground. Wood splintered.

With his tail between his legs, Bonbon fled the scene at a gallop.

"I got him, mister," Danny said.

"That's good, son. Don't let Ralph get away again."

Grady lowered the boy to the ground. His heart hammered in his chest. Jake Tyson, local villain, hadn't faired as well as Ralph. His leg was twisted at an awkward angle among the jumble that had once been a ladder.

In response to the commotion, local residents raced into the street. Grady knelt beside Jake's crumpled form just at the moment Jennifer appeared. The man's ruddy complexion had turned ashen and pain etched his face.

"It's broken," the man gasped, staring wide-eyed at his right leg that was twisted awkwardly through the rungs of the ladder. "I felt it snap." He lay his head back and looked up at the summer sky. "Sweet Jesus, if I can't work, who'll take care of Millie and the kids?"

Kneeling, Jennifer smoothed back the dark hair across his square forehead. "It's all right, Jake. Try not to worry. Millie will be fine and you won't have any money worries. The town will see to that."

Her soft, lyrical voice and gentle touch soothed the man. In spite of all that had happened, Grady had to admit deep in his gut he wished Jennifer would touch him like that.

"IT WAS MY FAULT," Grady said aloud a half hour later as the ambulance crew slammed the door shut on the van.

Self-consciously he dug into his wallet in response to the hat being passed to help Jake with expenses.

"Doesn't he have medical insurance?" Grady asked Jennifer.

"Probably not. He just works here and there at odd jobs, wherever he can. Unemployment is a real problem in the mountains, and a lot of families support themselves by cutting firewood because that's the only work they can find. But we'll get Jake's expenses covered."

"Hospital bills are enormous. You people can't—"

"Of course we can." She lifted her chin stubbornly. "Money is a commodity that's meant to be used when someone needs it, not just hoarded."

"I've never known a town that would—"

"Moraine is special. Good things happen here because people care. I tried to tell you that."

He jammed his hands in his pockets. There was something different about this town. He'd felt it from the beginning, though he couldn't quite define the reason. "Look, I feel like the accident was partly my fault. Maybe I can help with a few dollars more."

Her hair had come loose from its moorings. She flicked the golden strands behind her shoulder in a naturally graceful motion that made Grady ache to feel the silken threads draped across his bare chest.

"Don't bother, Mr. Murdock. You're set on destroying our town. The rest of it doesn't matter."

He'd never known anyone to turn down money, and it made him feel like a heel when she spun away to walk proudly up the street, her long skirt swaying with each footstep. She was a very determined lady. He liked that in a person, he admitted, though he hated the fact that she'd lied to him.

"Wait, Jenny." In two strides he caught up with her. "Look, I'm sorry I lost my temper." The last time he'd done that it had cost him a broken nose.

Her jaw squared, her back as rigid as a department store mannequin, she leveled Grady a determined look. "You don't have to feel guilty about the accident. You were trying to help Danny, and I appreciate that." Her manner was far less forgiving than her words.

"I admit I've got a really quick fuse," he confessed, noting that the haughty angle of her chin gave her a regal air…and would be a perfect place to plant a kiss. "Particularly when my male ego is involved."

She arched an eyebrow. "Ego?"

"Your talking me into playing the villain's part. And the way you've been acting. It was all very convincing." Particularly that onstage kiss. "I don't like to be the victim of a scam any more than the next guy. Everything you did was a lie."

"Not everything."

"Well, then, if you thought I was here to foreclose, why did you make up that hare-brained scheme? Why didn't you just ask me about my intentions?"

She stopped and stared at him blankly. "I don't know…. We all thought— It never occurred to anyone on the town council—"

"To be honest?"

"It's not that. You see…." She drew a deep breath that raised her breasts enticingly. "You see, all these buildings don't just represent businesses. They're our homes. To make the town into what we wanted, everyone deeded over their homes to the town council. Larry lives upstairs above his mercantile. The saloon keeper has his rooms in the back. Nyla has lived in her house all of her life. For all practical purposes, so have I.'' She chewed thoughtfully on her lower lip, and he remembered the velvety texture of her soft mouth on his.

''You could have told me,'' Grady suggested softly. He could see the town and its people were important to Jennifer. Maybe, just maybe, that justified a small lie...at least in her eyes.

''I suppose that would have been best.'' She sighed and found something interesting to study on the dusty toe of his Italian loafers. ''I guess we blew it.''

Something about Jennifer made her a very difficult woman to stay angry with. Grady discovered he didn't want to make the effort. ''Guess you won't be able to put on your melodrama this weekend without Jake.'' Now he knew what it felt like to be riddled with guilt.

''No. Unless...'' Her gaze slipped slowly up to meet his, and his heart knocked an extra beat. A suspicious smile lifted the corners of her mouth and her eyes sparkled with mischief. ''You're the kind of man who enjoys a challenge, aren't you, Grady?''

''Sometimes,'' he conceded. Like when he was closing in on a big deal...or pursuing a reluctant lady.

''Then *you* play the villain's part. For the weekend.''

He shook his head. ''I don't think so.''

"You said you wanted to do something more for Jake," she argued. "If we went ahead with the show we could ask for donations to cover his hospital bills and a little extra for the family to tide them over until he can get on his feet."

"Are you trying to con me again?"

Her smile was irresistible. Something told Grady he might have been better off if his guilty conscience had gone on vacation. Or perhaps the fates meant him to have one more fling on the stage.

On the other hand, he could easily rationalize staying in town to uncover why he'd been offered such a high return on the investors' money. That made a whole lot of sense.

Whatever the case, he accepted her challenge and nodded his agreement to playing the role of Pierre.

Jennifer felt a surge of relief. The show could go on. But that emotion was tempered with anxiety. She was experiencing a dangerous amount of curiosity about the man who affected her so strongly. "Why was your missing dollar so important to you?"

"It wasn't just any dollar. It was my lucky silver piece."

She cocked her head. "You're superstitious?"

"Of course not," he said abruptly. "I shouldn't have made such a big deal about it."

His tone made it clear he wasn't interested in pursuing the topic, and she didn't think she should pry.

After all of the earlier excitement, the street was now deserted. Jennifer felt very much at loose ends with an uncomfortable feeling she ought to get on with her own daily activities. Grady's presence was thoroughly unsettling. Three days of nervous tension stretched ahead of her.

He was such a take-charge kind of guy. His forcefulness, added to his incredible good looks, were hard to resist. It made the outlook for the weekend even more nerve-racking.

"As long as I'm going to be here for a couple of days," he said, as though reading her thoughts, "maybe you can help me figure out why a group of investors is so anxious to pick up the mortgages we're carrying."

"I can't imagine. The buildings are pretty rundown. We've done face-lifts but there's still a lot of structural work to be finished." Little rivulets of sweat edged down her neck, and she wiped them away. The heat, or perhaps Grady's nearness, was making her perspire.

"Let's get out of the sun," he suggested, his hand cupping her elbow. "Have there been any strangers around in the last couple of months asking questions?"

"I don't think so." He led her up onto the shaded boardwalk and she followed unquestioningly. His gesture was that of a confident male used to being in control of the situation. In control of women, too? she wondered anxiously and knew she shouldn't even be considering his personal relationships with the opposite sex. It was none of her business, she realized, fighting off an unwarranted twinge of jealousy.

"Has anyone been surveying the town lately?"

"No. I certainly would have heard about that. Besides, the town council passed some very strict ordinances. Any change has to be reviewed for historic authenticity. No one could come in with a grand plan for the town and hope to get approval."

He seated her on a wooden bench in front of the mercantile store, then sat on the railing opposite, his long, tapered fingers circling the rough wood. She hadn't noticed before how artistic his hands were. Remembering the feel of his hand, gentle, but forceful on her elbow, she shivered internally. She imagined the feel of his long fingers touching her more intimately, stroking and arousing her. So strong was the impression, her breathing accelerated and her nipples hardened with an unexpected ache.

Everything about Grady made her feel extraordinarily feminine and annoyingly vulnerable. She wondered if other women reacted quite so strongly to him and guessed that they did.

"How about the land around the town?" he asked. "Who owns that?"

Blinking to shut away her heated images, she said, "It's all national forest land. There's no logging here, though, because the altitude is too high for any significant timber stands."

"Then the forest service wouldn't think of it as very valuable?"

"I suppose not," she replied with a troubled frown, then fussed with her long skirt to let it fall more smoothly over her knees. She wished she could deal with Grady as easily as she did with every other man in Moraine. Friendly but not at all personal. But his eyes were different, dark and unreadable, his lips too finely chiseled, his smile too quick, his hands... She abruptly halted the recurring thought. "Isn't the forest service charged with taking care of wilderness areas whether or not there's logging?"

"Their motto is Land of Many Uses. That includes recreation. Maybe somebody's thinking about an upscale ski area."

"I hope not. Those ugly paths they cut through the trees." She shook her head. "Besides, we don't really get that much snow at this elevation. Some years almost none."

"Still, I think I ought to talk with the guy in charge of the forest."

"The headquarters is over in Sonora. The head ranger is a man named Charlie Wilson. I've had his son in a couple of my classes."

Balancing himself with his feet on the lower railing, Grady linked his hands together between his knees. Beneath his slacks, thigh muscles rippled. Jennifer found herself wondering what his legs looked like and if they were covered with the same dark hair that teased at the opened collar of his shirt.

With an effort she shifted her gaze back to his face, while her imagination perversely remained at a much lower elevation.

"This Wilson fella might be more willing to talk if you went with me, Jenny. Would you?"

Would a wise woman go anywhere alone with a villain? She doubted it. "Why don't you just call him? I'm sure he'd be happy to answer your questions."

"I find people talk more openly in person than they do on the phone. I'd like to get to the bottom of this."

She hesitated for a fractional beat. The thought of spending several hours alone with Grady made her nervous and caused her heart to beat a little faster. She didn't want to say yes.

But for her own peace of mind it was an opportunity she couldn't pass up. She would show him her world, the forests and streams she loved. He'd reject them with the same mocking tone that had cut her to the quick when she had described Moraine to Danny's father. Then it would be easy to put thoughts of Grady into a quiet niche and get on with her life.

Granted, there was some risk to her plan... both to herself and the town of Moraine. But it was a risk she would simply have to take.

"Yes, I'll go with you," she said, "if you'll agree I can show you the mountains my way."

Lifting a curious eyebrow, he shrugged his approval.

Chapter Six

"You're going to take your Porsche?"

Stepping away from Nyla's back porch where she'd been waiting, Jennifer stared in awe at the dark, flashy lines of the car, as sleek looking as its owner. And potentially just as dangerous.

He opened the door for her. "I never leave home without it."

"We're going the back way into town, Grady. My four-wheel drive would be—"

"Miserably uncomfortable." He patted the top of the car. "This little baby can go anywhere. Trust me."

Trust Grady Murdock? With what? Her heart. Her body. Just sitting still, his car looked like it was traveling a thousand miles an hour. She had the distinct feeling he was the kind of guy who moved way too fast for her. In everything he did.

Reluctantly she slid into the seat, and the soft cushions wrapped her in a sensuous embrace. "Don't say I didn't warn you if the road gets too rough." She'd be smarter to listen to the warning alarms in her own mind.

"You be the tour guide and leave the driving to me."

Grady settled comfortably behind the steering wheel. For the trip Jennifer had changed into jeans and a T-shirt. He liked how nicely the denim fabric tugged across her slender thighs and hugged the curve of her hips. She had good legs, he decided, in addition to other well-proportioned attributes that were more apparent than ever beneath her shirt.

"I'm sure you'll enjoy the scenery on this route," she said.

Grady thought he'd rather admire the scene of Jennifer's stenciled T-shirt molding to her firm breasts than a view of pine trees and mountain peaks. He might not be totally willing to trust her again, but the sight of her shapely body was definitely inspiring.

Grady wheeled onto the forest service road with complete confidence. Within a hundred feet, one wheel lurched into an unseen pothole. He cursed under his breath.

Good, Jennifer thought smugly. Grady was used to arrow-straight, eight-lane highways that were boring and unimaginative. In contrast she relished the back roads that snaked through the forest. She was simply experiencing a physical attraction to the man, she assured herself. They had nothing in common. Knowing that, she was sure her hormones would settle down soon.

She hoped.

"I take it you don't see any value in amenities like pavement?" he asked dryly.

"Highways are for people who don't know their way around the mountains."

"That sure includes me. This is only the second time I've ever been in the Sierras. The first was when I was a kid at Boy Scout Camp." With an expert flick of his wrist, he down-shifted and the car raced up a steep grade.

Jennifer felt her stomach do a flip-flop, and it was only partly because of the unsettling motion. The way Grady drove, and the way he made her feel, was like being on a wild roller coaster ride. Out of control.

"You obviously suffered through a deprived childhood," she said.

She gave him an uneasy smile and then turned her attention to the scenery. The road wove its way between lodge pole pines, and flashes of sunlight flicked across the windshield in an ever-changing pattern. Cuts in the hillside revealed iron-rich soil, casting the road in shades of red. On granite outcroppings, a painter's palette of brightly hued lichen formed a colorful, natural graffiti.

The sunlight moved across Grady's features, too, casting evocative shadows more exciting than any landscape she'd ever seen. Dark brows shaded his eyes; a bristle of afternoon whiskers shadowed his rugged jaw; a sturdy neck invited a woman to nuzzle her lips against his corded strength.

She silently observed the way his hands held the steering wheel, almost in a tender caress. Expertly he

stroked the vehicle through turn after turn, coaxing
the car around corners and over the roughest spots in
the road until the ride was a soaring experience, the
sunlight flashing past in a world of forest green. He
sensed intuitively when to accelerate and when to slow
and savor the moment. Muscles flexing slightly, his
movements were fluid and sure.

She imagined Grady Murdock would make love
with the same sort of care and confidence.

And she shouldn't be thinking about any of that.

"Didn't your family ever go camping on vacation?" she asked to distract herself.

He choked out a derisive laugh. "I can't remember
my father ever taking a vacation, at least not one that
wasn't part of a business trip, and my mother's idea of
fun is a four-star hotel or a cruise to the Caribbean. I
had to really work at it to get them to let me go to Boy
Scout Camp just that one summer."

"That's sad." But another of those reasons they
simply weren't right for each other, she realized, wondering why the confirmation of what she'd known all
along bothered her so much.

"Funny," Grady said, almost to himself. "My parents thought that Boy Scout Camp was a waste of
time. The next year they sent me to a special computer camp. Computer literacy seemed more important to them than the ability to tie a square knot and
put up a tent. The place was the pits. I had to stay
there the whole summer.

"Of course," Grady continued, a smile quirking his
lips, "the computer camp was co-ed. Sneaking a peek

in the girls' showers was at least a redeeming feature."

Jennifer swallowed a laugh. He'd probably been just as wickedly handsome as a boy as he was as a man. The girls must have been crazy about him.

Spying a deer just off the road up ahead, she placed her hand on Grady's arm. "Let's stop a minute to watch. Maybe her babies are around."

Responding to her gentle touch, Grady slowed the car to a stop.

Alerted, the deer eyed the vehicle suspiciously, her mulelike ears cupped for sounds of danger.

A surprising quiet enveloped the car. Something about those big, brown eyes and the deer's sleek coat plucked an unfamiliar chord within Grady, a feeling very primitive and basic.

Oddly, within the confines of his Porsche, Grady felt a kinship to cavemen who had looked out on their world. He had a woman to protect, though from no great threat at the moment.

He shook his thoughts aside. It was one thing to be attracted to a nineteenth-century woman. If he began to think of himself as a caveman, Jennifer might not be impressed by his actions, which would surely include tossing her over his shoulder and hauling her off to some secluded spot. Maybe to a cave, he mused, wondering what it would be like to make love with Jennifer on a bearskin rug.

He could almost see her honey-blond hair spread in wild abandon across the darker fur of the rug and the contrast of her porcelain skin against the deep backdrop. Her lips would be slightly parted, her eyes aglow with desire, and he would be able to admire every delectable inch of her.

Enticing idea.

This mountain air had certainly stimulated his imagination, Grady realized, adjusting himself to a more comfortable position. Not like him at all.

He cleared his throat only to have Jennifer hush him with a quick gesture.

"There're her babies," she whispered. Two fawns, still spotted with white splotches, joined their mother, and then the three of them ambled across the road.

When the trio had vanished into the woods, Jennifer sighed and gave Grady a radiant smile that made her eyes glisten. "Aren't they beautiful?"

"Beautiful?" He draped his arm around the back of her seat and let his fingers play with the tips of her silken hair. "I didn't notice. I was too busy watching you. You're the most lovely sight in the woods, as far as I'm concerned."

A soft, half smile tilted her rosy lips. "Grady, I'm supposed to be showing you the countryside."

"You're doing a fine job."

Jennifer's eyes widened at the husky, intimate timbre of his voice. A shiver scuttled down her spine.

Even if she'd wanted to speak, she didn't think she could. Not right then. She could feel his fingers tangling in her hair, tugging gently. The feeling was unexpectedly erotic, the look in his eyes quite mesmerizing. It was as though he'd discovered a new, masculine fascination with something as simple as her hair. Strangely, it gave her a sense of power she'd never before experienced.

"I think . . ." The lump in her throat didn't want to budge. "There's something else . . . down the road I'd like to show you." She purposefully removed his arm from the back of her seat and placed his hand on the steering wheel. "Beaver Tooth Pond."

"Sounds delightful."

"One of my favorite places." *Much safer than sitting so close to you.*

A half mile later, Grady pulled the car off to the side of the road as instructed.

"I didn't mean for this project to take all afternoon," Grady protested when Jennifer climbed out of the car.

"It won't take long," she assured him. "I like to check on the neighbors once in a while."

Beavers for neighbors? At least they didn't have raucous, late-night parties, Grady conceded.

Jennifer squatted down on the slick, muddy bank. The crystal-clear water reflected the sky and the row of pine trees on the opposite shore in a shimmer of blue and green. An osprey nest of jumbled twigs perched precariously in the leafless branches of the tallest tree. With a sigh Jennifer let the midday silence of the forest embrace her.

This wasn't the sort of place a man like Grady could enjoy. There was no hustle or bustle, no deals to be made. He'd be miserable in the solitude, yet for her this was part of the attraction of the mountains. For a moment she regretted putting him through the ordeal just to prove to herself they weren't suited for each other.

She ought to get back into the car and have him drive straight through to Sonora.

No way, she decided, on second thought. She enjoyed seeing the beavers and she wasn't going to miss this chance just because Grady was getting impatient.

"We have to call to the beavers by slapping a shoe on the bank," she explained. "If they're home, they'll come out to investigate."

"And invite us in to tea?"

She scowled at him. He stood by the side of the car looking as though he wasn't even going to try to enjoy the experience.

Taking off her sandal, she slapped it a half dozen times against the mud.

When nothing happened after a few moments, she tried again.

"You try it, Grady," Jennifer called. "The soles of your shoes are thicker than mine. The mother beaver is sure to be around. She had a big litter this spring. Four kits."

"I'm not exactly dressed for tramping through the woods."

"Does the thought of getting muddy bother you that much?" she challenged. It's what she'd expected.

She stood, only to discover Grady walking toward her, unconcerned by the blades of damp grass marking his slacks. Her mouth hung open.

At the edge of the pond he gingerly removed his right shoe and tried to balance himself on one foot while bending over from the waist. His perch was very precarious on the slippery bank.

"Be careful," she warned.

The bank moved beneath his foot. He tried to regain his balance with his stockinged foot but it was too late. The mud and dirt crumbled under his weight. With a splash, he went into the water.

Jennifer gasped, "Oh, dear," and covered her mouth with her hand. Poor Grady looked ever so foolish sitting in two feet of water with all of his carefully tailored clothes on, his one dry shoe still held safely above his head. Her cheek muscles ached trying to prevent a grin. She hadn't meant for him to get soaked just so she could prove a point.

"Do you need help?" Muffled laughter made her voice ripple like the surface of the pond.

"That would be nice." He tossed his remaining shoe onto the bank. "How 'bout a hand?"

The moment Grady grasped her wrist, Jennifer knew she'd made a disastrous mistake by laughing at him. He had that amused glint in his eye that told her very clearly he was about to get even. Like a playful schoolboy, it was pigtail-in-the-inkwell time. She was the intended victim.

"No, Grady, don't! I don't want to get wet."

"The water's fine. Very refreshing."

"I'll take your word for it."

"You thought it was pretty funny when I fell in."

"But that was an accident," Jennifer objected. Why didn't he let go of her? And why did she enjoy watching lighthearted amusement play across his features, bringing crinkles to the corners of his eyes? For the moment he didn't seem at all villainous. Just fun to be with.

She hadn't had much time for playful moments in her life lately. She loved raising Danny and trying to make Moraine a financial success, but she missed having a man in her life...and bed.

With a quick, agile movement and a determined gleam in his eye, Grady was on his feet, scooping her into his arms.

She squealed and struggled, kicking her feet uselessly in the air, her sandals flying off.

"Easy now. I wouldn't want to drop you." He waded slowly through the water toward the deeper part of the pond.

His grin was sexy and seductive, sending little rivulets of excitement through Jennifer. Beneath his damp shirt she could feel the heat of his flesh and the way his muscles flexed with each step. He was hardness and strength, more virile than she'd realized. There was nothing vulnerable about him. He was definitely a man in charge.

Helpless to struggle further, she clung to him, burying her face at the crook of his neck and smelling the musky base note of his skin. This wasn't working out right at all, she thought with a groan. A plan gone dangerously wrong.

"I don't think I'm going to like this," she said through clenched teeth as mountain-cooled water lapped at her toes.

"Trust me, my precocious pretty," he said in Pierre's lecherous voice. "I mean you no harm."

"The heck you don't," she gasped. The way he cradled her was carefully designed to press her breasts hard against his chest, doing dangerous things to her pulse rate. It took her breath away.

With a sharp stab of awareness, she realized she liked being in Grady's arms. Wanton sensations sparked through her body. She wanted to be held; she desired however many kisses he might offer. The urgency of this newly discovered need stunned her with its intensity.

"Careful now," he said.

She heard huskiness in his voice as he released her legs and lowered her slowly along the length of his body, inching her into the pond. She was acutely conscious of the feel of his broad chest, the flatness of his stomach. Her body molded naturally against his. Where she was soft, he was as solid as an oak. Her fingers dug into the bunched muscles of his arms. His potent virility overwhelmed her senses.

After the first shock of cold water seeped through her jeans, she became aware of the gentle current brushing around her legs and between her thighs, as soft as a lover's caress. Wavelets lapped at her waist, sending shivers up her spine.

She imagined Grady's tapered fingers stroking her in the same way the water did—at the tender spot behind her knees, on the sensitive flesh of her thighs, and at the apex of her legs where the folds of her womanhood were moist and waiting.

Her toes touched the muddy bottom of the pool. She slipped a little and Grady pulled her closer. His gentle grip on her buttocks and the pressure of his arousal firmly against her abdomen spoke eloquently of an awakened need that matched her own riotous desire.

She closed her eyes against the dizzying sensations swirling around her. Masculine heat. The branding press of his hands. Sweet-smelling breath brushing her cheek. The feel of his heart beating hard against her chest.

His hands slid to her midriff, his fingers nearly circling her waist. In spite of the cold water, his touch was warm, sending glittering flames of desire to lick through her body. She drew a quick breath that fed the fire.

As though by design, his thumbs pressed into the lower curve of her breasts. Did he know what she was feeling? The scorching sensation each time his hand slicked against her flesh?

She swallowed a groan. Of course he knew exactly what he was doing to her. And she didn't want him to stop.

The cold water cooled her flesh while at her inner core her temperature rose by steady degrees. She shuddered and tried futilely to recall all the ways in which they were totally wrong for each other. For the moment not a single thought came to mind.

"Ah, my sweet Jenny. Together we're fire and ice. I can feel you melting." His lips sought the column of her neck. "Can you feel it, too?"

From the inside out. "I don't think I'm ready..."

"You will be. In time."

A heated shiver curled through her stomach. A frighteningly languorous feeling threatened to take over all reason, all thought. A languid heat attacked her limbs as well as her mind. She desperately sought some way to halt the weakening of her defenses in the face of Grady's determined onslaught of sensual signals.

Almost with relief she spotted a silvery arrow of water across the pond.

"Grady, I think we have company."

His right hand moved to more fully encompass her breast. "Tell 'em to go find their own pond."

She drew a shuddering breath. "They have. We're in it."

"Uh-umm." He didn't sound in the least interested.

"The beavers. They're watching us."

Startled, he turned suddenly. His feet slipped on the muddy, uneven bottom of the pond. His legs snaked around her knees.

In a flurry of arms and legs, they both went fully into the water.

Jennifer came up sputtering and laughing.

"My hero!" she sighed dramatically. "Done in by a beaver."

"They should have minded their own business." He finger-combed the rakish lock of hair that had fallen across his forehead. A predatory smile canted his lips in a way that suggested they hadn't quite finished what had been started.

"Come on, big guy. I think we've worn out our welcome." And she'd handled about all of the stress she could manage for the moment. She started to swim away.

He caught her by the hand. "Not so fast."

Drawn back to him like a bird in a snare, she found herself pressed against his broad chest once again. Heat flamed through the pit of her stomach for a second time. The determined seduction blazing in his dark eyes left her weak and trembling. His gaze settled on her mouth, lingering there as her breathing quickened. Vibrant desire haloed him in colors so shockingly bright they seared into her soul.

"The beaver can wait," he insisted hoarsely.

He ensnared the back of her head with his long, tapered fingers. With another hungry look for warning, he lowered his mouth on hers.

Hot talons of need sank through her flesh. Instinctively her arms wrapped themselves around Grady's shoulders. Her fingers laced through the warm, damp coils of his hair. Heat burned through her until she thought the beaver pond might boil away. She was no ice maiden now. Molten lava raced through her veins.

His leg pressed between her thighs, excruciatingly intimate and enticingly exciting.

She rode the wave of desire that swept over her. Her awareness scattered to a dozen points of contact—his tongue toying with hers, the press of his leg, his hands cupping, stroking in the most intimate of ways. All of the sensations brought on a madness of need she still had enough sense to resist.

"Enough," she said. Her voice was little more than a sultry whisper against his mouth.

"I doubt it will ever be enough," he warned softly. "Fire can always melt ice."

She pressed her palms to his chest with little conviction.

"Sooner or later, sweet Jenny, I'm going to have you."

She shook her head.

"Count on it." He gently released her to float away.

With muscles gone nerveless, she scissor-kicked to shore and struggled up the bank. She felt as though she'd crossed twenty miles of open ocean. Sinking to the ground, she gasped for breath. What insanity had overtaken her? She imagined she would be able to feel the warm imprint of Grady's body against hers all the rest of her life.

She kept her eyes glued to the ground while she caught her breath. It was bad enough knowing Grady had experienced a desire for her in the pond. She was terrified he might see in her eyes that she had been equally aroused. She still felt a fullness to her breasts and a throbbing warmth between her thighs. The pulse at her throat continued to beat a slow, heavy rhythm.

Their whole relationship had subtly changed. Perhaps not so subtly, she reconsidered, but it had certainly become infinitely more complicated.

Grady swept the water from his hair and followed more slowly out of the pond. Lust was a familiar experience for him. He knew how to handle that.

But what he'd felt with Jennifer in his arms was quite different. She was so soft, so pliable, simple lust would have been worse than an insult. He couldn't give his feelings a name but he knew he wanted more from Jennifer than an easy mating of man with woman.

Only her veneer was icy, prim and proper, he realized. He wanted her hot in his arms, as passionate as he knew her to be.

Looking down at her as she sat on the muddy bank, he deliberately studied her drenched appearance. Now that, he decided, is how a woman ought to wear a T-shirt. Soaking wet. Her nipples were hard little nubs pressing against the fabric. He could almost taste their dusty-rose flavor. Someday soon he would.

Chapter Seven

"If we're going to see your friend in Sonora," Grady said, "we'd better get changed."

Jennifer's head snapped up. "Changed?"

"Sure. I've got my tennis shorts in the trunk, and I always carry a clean white shirt. Just in case."

Just in case of what? Jennifer wondered. An unexpected overnight stay with a girlfriend? Probably.

As Grady walked to the car, Jennifer twisted the water from her long hair. She must look a fright, she thought. Grady looked more gorgeous than any man had a right.

After their dip in the pond, he was no longer so precision pressed and somehow more approachable, less threatening. That was a frightening thought. She shouldn't be considering how much fun it was to spend time with Grady Murdock; she shouldn't have visions of Sunday afternoon drives through the woods and secluded mountain pools where they could be alone. Thoughts of swimming naked together shouldn't be skittering through her head, or how she'd like to make love with Grady Murdock on the sunlit bank of a mountain stream.

But that's exactly what she was thinking—not with her head but with her molten inner core he'd discovered so expertly.

"I've got a towel, too," Grady announced, returning to her side and kneeling next to her. "Here, I'll dry your hair."

"That's all right. I can manage." Keeping her distance from Grady was a much smarter idea.

"Nonsense. I'm the one who dropped you in the water. The least I can do is help dry you off."

"You really don't have to..." The terry cloth provided little barrier between his powerful fingers and her scalp. He kneaded gently. Tingles of new awareness radiated from each spot he touched, as though her blood were racing helter-skelter to welcome him.

"You're hair is so thick and luxuriant I don't think the towel can do the whole job." He lifted the weight of her hair and dragged the soft toweling back and forth across her neck.

Sparks of desire spread along the path he blazed. "We'll keep the car windows down the rest of the way to Sonora." She swallowed hard. "It's a warm day." About five hundred degrees, if she were to go by the sheen of perspiration that suddenly dotted her forehead, and the dryness of her mouth.

"Okay. That's the best I can do for the moment. Take off your shirt and bra."

She went rigid. "What?"

"My dress shirt will be way too big for you, but at least you'll be dry on top."

"Grady, I usually dress in private."

He tugged the bottom of her damp T-shirt up to her midriff, his hands hot on her cold flesh. "The beavers won't mind."

"But I mind."

"I promise if they peek I'll send them home." He slipped one of her arms out of the sleeve.

"I'm more worried about you." And what you're doing to me.

Her other arm worked free. "I've got my eyes closed," he said in a low, rusty voice.

Scooting out of his reach, Jennifer stood. "Liar. If you'll just give me the shirt, I'll find a nice, thick bush for a dressing room."

A predatory smile curled his lips and crinkled the corners of his eyes. "Whatever you say, Ms. Sweetham. For now."

Her lungs spasmed in the search for air. She snatched the shirt from his hand, spun around and fled into the still forest.

Safely out of sight behind a tree, Jennifer did the best she could to turn the oversized shirt into something respectable to wear by knotting the long tail at her waist. Calming her heart rate was a high priority, too, which she just barely managed.

When she returned to the pond she found Grady pulling a white and pale blue knitted shirt over his head. She caught a quick glimpse of his dark chest hair arrowing its way beneath the snug waistband of his tennis shorts.

The sight brought a catch to her throat.

Lord, he was the most virile man she'd ever seen.

And his legs. Muscular thighs, tight calves, all covered by the same dark, curling hair that begged for a woman's touch. She imagined doing just that—feeling his hair-roughened calves with her palm, scoring his thighs with her fingernails and searching for his velvet manhood she knew nested, waited, among his hidden curls.

She clenched her hands to block the sensation from her mind.

He eyed her from ten feet away, his insolent gaze slowly perusing her with such intimacy it felt like the brush of his hand on her flesh. Or the touch of his lips. He was a man who knew just what he wanted, she mused, and just how to go about getting it. For the moment he seemed to want her.

Never taking his eyes from her, he brushed a lock of his damp hair back from his forehead. "No bra?"

"It was . . . wet."

"I imagine so." His velvet tone dragged across her skin.

She folded her arms in self-defense. "Shall we be on our way?"

AN HOUR LATER the Porsche finally lurched up onto the concrete highway near Sonora.

"The back way certainly isn't a shortcut," Grady observed. "Must have taken us three hours."

Jennifer gave him a dismissive shrug. "I make it a point to go that way at least once a week, just to watch the seasonal changes. If I had the time, I'd probably never go on the highway."

"I don't often have time to travel the back routes."

"Then you miss a lot."

Perhaps he did, Grady silently conceded, though he had rather mixed emotions about their jaunt through the woods. In some ways, his unplanned dip in the natural pool had been far more invigorating than a long soak in a hot spa.

With a puzzled twist of his lips, he realized his comparison between a mountain pool and a spa was not an original thought. He'd read it, heard it, somewhere else. Oddly it seemed important to remember where, but nothing came to mind. He was too keyed up, on edge, too aware of Jennifer and the hours they'd spent together, to give any problem serious consideration. That in itself was seriously troubling. He'd never had difficulty concentrating on his work.

Until now.

Knowing Jennifer wasn't wearing a bra was driving him crazy. He actually envied his damn shirt for the way it rested softly against her breasts, just where he'd like to pillow his head.

All in due time, he told himself, trying to ignore the determined ache in his groin.

Jennifer finger-combed her hair into some semblance of order as she watched pedestrians cross in front of the car.

As soon as they'd arrived in town, she'd felt the usual jolt of adjustment to the more frantic pace of Sonora compared to her home in Moraine. While hardly metropolitan, few people smiled at one another as they passed. She searched the street for familiar cars and faces, for friends who were like family. Inching along with the traffic toward the single signal in the center of town, she felt her discomfort mounting.

The sidewalks were jammed with tourists checking racks of T-shirts displayed outside small shops. Sporting goods stores vied for attention with gift shops and antique stores. Beyond the edge of town there was a new shopping center, frequented by the burgeoning population, and a couple of fast-food franchises that added the aroma of fried hamburgers to air already tainted by gasoline fumes.

If someone was planning a big development for Moraine, her little town would change in the way she'd watched Sonora alter over the years. Progress? She wasn't so sure.

Like a cord tightening around her chest, she realized Grady would take the opposite view. The crux of their differences lay in their basic values. Because of his job, money had to be a high priority for him. The gulf between them was still as wide as two distant peaks, no matter how much he might desire her physically. She couldn't let down her guard. She didn't dare.

"Do you like your work?" she asked, knowing the answer.

"I'm pretty good at what I do," he answered unself-consciously. "I've had clients who've made thousands of dollars because I've picked out spectacular investments for them. I apparently inherited the knack of knowing what's going to work financially, and I'm proud of that. It's a gut instinct that works."

"But do you ever take time to have fun like we did this afternoon?"

He searched for an answer. "Well, I . . ."

"That's what I thought." She pointed at the forest service headquarters office, and Grady paused to wait for oncoming traffic before making a left turn.

"Now just what do you mean by that remark?"

"I mean, Grady, that people don't know how to have fun anymore. They dig themselves into an early grave with nothing but work." She drew a deep breath that raised her shirt in a holier-than-thou way that both irritated and delighted Grady. "Moraine is about people creating their own fun."

Grady didn't want to acknowledge how close to home her remarks had struck. Fourteen-hour days were standard for him. "I enjoyed your personalized lesson at the beaver pond," he said, raising his eyebrows suggestively. "It was a hell of a lot more entertaining than the last Super Bowl."

She blew out a frustrated breath. "I didn't mean that kind of fun."

"All right, Miss High-and-Mighty, just how is the town of Moraine going to change the world? Are you really so innocent you'd think—"

"I'm not naive, Grady. I tried the fast track. It didn't work for me. Moraine and what we have there isn't just different. It's better."

He wanted to yell at her, but something about the intensity of her emotion plucked at an envious chord buried deeply within him. Was there anything in his life he cared about as much as Jennifer cared about her town?

"If we're going to change the world we have to do it one child at a time," she said, turning to face him, the tilt of her chin stubborn and determined. "Moraine caters to children, but in a much different way than an amusement park. Every adult tourist has to be accompanied by a child or they aren't allowed in the town. Then our kids take over. Danny's terrific at teaching kids how to roll a hoop. We've got some boys who teach marbles and all of the girls play jacks. They corner every youngster who comes into town, and by the time the child goes home he knows how to entertain himself for hours. Good, healthy fun."

Grady was skeptical. "Are you trying to tell me that after you get a hold of them, they'd give up a trip to Disneyland for a chance to play marbles?"

"Well, probably not. But they do learn they have their own internal resources. Moraine becomes their town, not a creation of adults, and then anything is possible."

"Interesting concept but it doesn't strike me as very lucrative. I have to confess it was one of my staff people who touted Moraine as an investment. I wasn't so sure."

Jennifer let out another exasperated sigh. "You'll see what I mean this weekend."

CHARLIE WILSON reached across the reception counter, taking both of Jennifer's hands in his bear-like paws. His weather-lined face cracked into a broad smile. "Good to see you, Jen. What brings you to town to mix with all the tourists?"

"Business." Standing on tiptoe, she leaned across the counter to kiss his rough cheek. "This is Grady Murdock..." How should she introduce him? For a moment at the pond they were very close to being lovers. Which, of course, was entirely impossible with the future of Moraine in his hands. "He's, ah, looking for some information."

"Sure. What do you need to know?"

Shaking hands with the head ranger, Grady said, "I've heard some rumors about possible developments in the Moraine area. We thought you might have had some building requests submitted, or maybe just heard some talk around?"

Charlie looked doubtful. "A movie company wants to do a shoot, up by Pine Crest."

"Probably something bigger. And permanent."

"Nothing comes to mind." Charlie lifted a part of the counter to allow them access. "Come on in and I'll let you look at the files. It's all public record."

Jennifer followed the two men into Charlie's office.

As she watched them examining the files, Jennifer was struck by the way Charlie deferred to Grady. It was as though even without being told, Charlie knew the man in his office was important, that he had influence. Grady exuded power and self-confidence. In a way she envied him that. It was also very intimidating. Grady was used to getting what he wanted.

At the beaver pond, he'd wanted her. At least he'd desired her physically. In her experience, men like Grady played games she didn't like.

She stiffened her spine. This was her turf. She would somehow have to keep that in mind. Even so, she found herself fascinated by the way his water-dampened hair swirled in waves across the back of his head, this way and that, mussed by cowlicks she'd like to comb smooth with her fingers.

Odd how she couldn't get over this persistent urge to touch Grady—in a thousand different ways. It was as though she needed to learn every peak and valley of his muscular body so she would have the memories to savor for the rest of her life.

Concentrating on his investigation, Grady thumbed through the green government forms. There were a couple of requests for vacation homes and a good many denied requests for cutting timber. Nothing that he'd call major in the way of development. "What's this one all about?" Grady asked, pointing at one of the forms.

Charlie peered through his reading glasses. "Just some water company checking back-country quality. Doesn't say why. Maybe they're thinking about bottling something like mountain Perrier water. Designer waters are supposed to be real big now."

"You're right." Grady fingered the smudged government form. He'd read something about the recent fad. "Big profit return on water these days." It didn't have the smell of big development that he would have expected. Though maybe somebody had discovered beaver pond water had aphrodisiac properties. Now *that* would be worth a bundle. And he'd be in line to buy the first bottle.

"You know, Mr. Murdock, most of the negotiations for alternative land uses usually occur way above my level. This is all pretty routine stuff. The head honchos at regional, or even national, would be more likely to see something like that than I would."

"I suppose you're right." Grady closed up the file and handed it back to Charlie. "Could you do a little asking around for me? Discreetly, if you can?"

"For a friend of Jenny? You bet."

Thanking the ranger, Grady wondered why the proposed development was such a damned tight little secret. Must be they didn't have all their ducks in a row just yet.

"Sorry your trip to town was wasted," Jennifer said as they came back out onto the sidewalk.

"Maybe Wilson will come up with something after he checks around." Grady knew researching any problem took time. He just wished he could connect some of the fragments of ideas he'd had all day. He was decidedly unfocused. Or maybe focused too hard on Jennifer. The beaver pond water certainly had long-lasting effects.

"You know what I'd like to do?" he asked, glancing up and down the street.

"What's that?"

"When I was at the Boy Scout Camp I told you about, we stopped somewhere—I have no idea what town we were in—and had the best chocolate-walnut-cherry ice cream I've ever had in my life."

"You're kidding."

"That the Boy Scouts took us for ice cream?"

"No, that you like chocolate-walnut-cherry."

"Sure, but they probably don't make it anymore. It's been years since I—"

"Edelman's Parlor. South of town. It's where we always go and I always have—I think it's the only place in the world where you can get chocolate-walnut-cherry. They make it themselves."

He cocked his head. "It's your favorite, too?"

She nodded, her delight making her eyes sparkle.

"I'll be damned." He hooked his arm through hers. "Come on, Ms. Sweetham. My treat."

THE ICE-CREAM PARLOR was an eclectic cross between an 1890s historic scene and a 1950 muscle-car haven. Customers sat on white wrought iron chairs at glass tables while the walls were covered with memorabilia of old Fords and Chevies, including the whole back end, fins and all, of a '57. On the mezzanine, electronic games roared and pinged, fed by youngsters shoving quarters into the slots as fast as they could go.

"This is great," Grady announced, scooping up the last big bite of his ice cream.

"You shouldn't have put chocolate sauce on it," Jennifer admonished with a smile. "Ruins the flavor and makes it too rich."

Laughing, Grady pointed out, "Your marshmallow sauce is just as sweet."

"Maybe." Jennifer had eaten only about half of her heaping dish of ice cream. She'd been idly wondering if you could base an entire relationship with a man on the fact that you both loved the same kind of ice cream. It seemed doubtful. But it was a relief to know they shared the same taste in something.

It was the burning look in Grady's dark eyes that snatched her reason away. Her breasts had developed a persistent tingle; her breathing was decidedly shallow. Her stomach and her heart kept trying to change places. When her knee had accidentally brushed against Grady's under the table, she'd felt an electric jolt right between her thighs.

Even in a room full of customers, the feeling of intimacy was claustrophobic.

"We should be getting back to Moraine," she suggested. "We have the rehearsal—"

"We'll leave soon." Grady tipped his chair back and crossed his arms contentedly across his chest.

There was a little drop of chocolate at the corner of his mouth. Jennifer knew how sweet it would taste. Wanted to lick it off. And wished she'd stop thinking like that.

"Tell me about Charlie Wilson," he asked. "You seemed to know him pretty well. More than just the father of one of your students. Will he be honest with me if he finds out anything from topside?"

His tongue flicked along the edge of his lips to sweep the chocolate drop away, and she felt a tremor of longing.

"Charlie's absolutely honest. He's one of my all-time favorite people. I owe him a lot."

"How's that?"

She hesitated, stirring her spoon through the melted ice cream in her dish. She and Charlie Wilson had gone through some difficult times together. "When I applied for the teaching job at Sonora High the school board president objected to their hiring me."

"Why would anyone object to you?"

"Mrs. Phillips, the president, is a good person, I suppose. It's just that..." Jennifer struggled for words. "Oh, hell, she's a nosy old busybody who'd do bed checks on every teenager in the county if they'd let her. She thinks her whole mission in life is to guard the morality of our kids. *Straitlaced* doesn't even begin to describe her."

"And she didn't want you teaching? That doesn't make any sense."

"Remember me? I'm the local fallen woman. Unforgivable, as far as Mrs. Phillips was concerned."

"What century is she living in?"

"You've got to understand, Mrs. Phillips is very influential in this county. She's a political animal, however misdirected some of her views might be. She sees herself and Sonora as the center of the universe. Anyone from the outlying 'villages' like Moraine is a peasant. Charlie Wilson has been one of our neighbors for years and was on the school board at the time. He stood nose to nose with her and convinced a majority of the board that I wouldn't lead the schoolchildren to rack and ruin." She wadded her napkin into a tight ball.

"Good for Charlie." Grady held up his thumb in salute.

"It cost him the next election. Phillips put up her own candidate and ran a really dirty campaign against Charlie. He's always told me he hated the aggravation, anyway, but I've never quite believed him. He took his job very seriously. I think he was hoping he could change things."

Grady let his chair settle back on all four legs. He loved Jennifer's intensity. Charlie Wilson must have felt just as strongly about sticking up for a woman's rights. For a moment Grady hated that his parents hadn't taught him to care about something besides rate of return and the New York Stock Exchange. Maybe then he'd understand Jennifer better and could find the key to unlock her passion for him.

"I guess living in a small town where everybody knows your business has its disadvantages," he said.

"In a way. You get so close it's like they're all in your back pocket." She laughed without bitterness. "There's no way to keep a secret here. But that just means everyone has to be themselves. Nobody's phony. What you see is what you get."

Leaning forward, he said, "Whatever ol' Mrs. Phillips thinks, I'll bet you're a damned good teacher."

She grinned. "The best."

Chapter Eight

Grady pushed his way through the Founder's Day crowd. "Big doings" were already in full swing.

Glancing across the street, he spotted Jennifer in the crowd. He drew in a quick breath. She looked like a spring flower in yellow and white, her long gown cut low at the neck, the fair skin of her shoulders shaded by a matching parasol. In comparison, the rest of the townspeople looked faded by the summer sun.

For a moment he silently observed her. Her pert nose. A determined chin lifted with a mixture of pride and defiance. Lips that were naturally rosy and sensuous, so kissable it made him ache for her. An innocent face framed by golden curls.

Her sweet face and modest costume were no more than an alluring mask to hide the sexy lady hidden somewhere inside, he realized. He'd come close at the beaver pond to releasing the depths of her passion. He sensed that like an underground stream her feelings ran deep. The guy who could uncover her secret desires would have one hell of a lady on his hands—and in his bed.

Slowly she turned. He met her gaze, his brown eyes dueling with the blue eyes framed in her heart-shaped face. The corners of her mouth lifted into a smile, both heart stopping and seductive. He wondered if she had any idea what she could do to a man.

Then her expression closed, like a morning glory when a cloud passes overhead, and she looked anxiously around the crowd as though she was seeking somewhere to hide. She nervously twisted the handle of her parasol.

A reluctant lady, Grady thought, crossing to her side of the street. Quite a challenge.

"You're a late sleeper," she said, a trace of anxiety in her eyes. "You've already missed the horse race."

"Not really," he replied dryly. "From the sounds I heard I figure they ran it right through my bedroom."

His heart registered her silver laughter, bright and shiny and new. He had an urge to take her in his arms and kiss her but knew she'd object in front of all these people. So would he, if he had any good sense left at all. Which apparently he didn't since he leaned toward her to brush her lips with his.

The simple contact jolted him and it had nothing to do with static electricity. He lingered a moment enjoying the heated sparks that leapt between them.

Feel the fire, Jenny, he telegraphed with the quick penetration of his tongue. You can't hide your passion from me.

When he withdrew, her eyes were wide with surprise, as though she'd felt the same high-powered voltage and heard his message loud and clear.

Her tongue darted out to lick her lips and he had to stifle a groan. God, he wanted to taste her again.

Jennifer wrapped her fingers more tightly around her parasol. Lord, it was hard to keep her equilibrium whenever Grady was around. He had a diabolical ability to catch her off guard, which she didn't seem able to fight. No other man had ever had that effect on her. Not by a long shot.

From the moment she'd seen him in his signature sport shirt and carefully pressed slacks she'd felt herself on that breathless roller coaster ride again. He was the most devilishly attractive tourist in town.

That thought brought her up short. He should be wearing . . .

"Grady, since you're a member of the melodrama cast . . ." She shifted her parasol to shade her eyes. "Would you mind wearing a costume today?"

"You mean a black suit and that awful top hat from the play?"

"Well, no, you wouldn't have to go that far. But maybe we could find you something suitable at the mercantile. Something Western?"

He chuckled. "You want me in cowboy boots?"

Actually, a black shirt and hip-hugging jeans were more what she had in mind for the resident villain. The image fit. "Let's take a look at what Larry has at the store. We have time before the hoop-rolling contest starts."

"Ah, yes. The kids were training for the event when I arrived." He offered his arm. "Let's get our shopping done. Wouldn't want to miss the race."

A few minutes later Grady had made his choices from the mercantile's Western selections, and they were back out on the street.

He settled his new black Stetson squarely on his head. The brim shadowed his dark eyes. "Now then, Ms. Sweetham . . ." He twisted the tip of his mustache between his finger and thumb, giving her an illicit look intended to suggest the most evil of intentions. "About the mortgage. In lieu of foreclosure, let's negotiate."

She felt the tight thrill of forbidden attraction. "And what, kind sir, did you have in mind?" she asked, as though his desire were not entirely too obvious.

His gaze briefly settled on her lips then slid to the swell of her breasts, creating a tingling sensation as if he had actually touched her. "Perhaps a kiss would serve to open the discussion. Then later, my dear, I shall take great pleasure in ravishing your lovely—"

"Grady! Someone will hear you." She laughed a nervous, high-pitched sound. He was trying to seduce her right here on a crowded street. And doing a good job of it, too. "Come on. The hoop race—"

"Jennifer, you cut me to the quick. To think you'd forgo the pleasures we might enjoy together for something as mundane as a hoop race. 'Tis a great weight of misery we villains must carry." His face canted into a silly grin that was even more seductive than his villain's leer. "Then again, perhaps I need a new script writer."

"I'll check the writer's union first thing Monday morning." And find somebody to write her out of the script. Just being around Grady, she was playing with fire.

Grady cocked his elbow and she slipped her arm through his.

"I trust we haven't missed the lizard race," he said. Her hand was as light as a dandelion seed on his arm and as intoxicating as wine.

"Don't worry. We save the best for last."

Closing his hand over hers, he said softly, "I'd say I've already found the best there is."

Her hand trembled slightly in response.

In another minute he was going to be spouting Shakespearean sonnets. Definitely not his style. He must have left his hard-boiled businessman facade outside the barricade at the edge of town. Or maybe wearing cowboy boots did that to a man.

Joining the milling crowd, they strolled slowly down Main Street and Grady caught the faint violet scent of her perfume. He suspected even in another lifetime the fragrance would always remind him of the woman who now held his arm so tightly.

Jennifer had to force one foot in front of the other. She always felt slightly out of balance when Grady was near.

It was as though he could effortlessly reach inside to find all the barriers she'd carefully built and brush them away as easily as a flooding river erodes loose sand. Like a swimmer caught in the current, she was losing ground with each stroke. She had the ominous feeling that somewhere downstream there was a dangerous waterfall.

This time she wouldn't be the only one to suffer. Danny would be hurt, too. He'd still been talking about Grady at breakfast.

"He's neat, Mom, almost as good as Billy's dad," Danny had insisted that morning. "Can he go campin' with us, Mom? Can he?"

"He's only here for the weekend. For the play."

"You could invite him back. He'd come. I know he would. I could teach him to fish 'n' stuff."

How could Danny have developed an attachment to Grady so quickly? she wondered. Maybe rescuing lizards did that for a man, came the answer loud and clear.

From out of the Founder's Day crowd Smitty Guterra, the local barber, startled Jennifer by grabbing her affectionately by the arm. Dressed as a miner and carrying a bird cage containing a canary, he demanded to meet Grady.

"How ya like our little town?" Smitty asked, pumping Grady's hand as though he were trying to raise water from five hundred feet down. "Great place, eh? Wouldn't want nuthin' to change here. No, sir, not one little thing."

"Nary a feather?" Grady replied.

"That's the spirit, ol' buddy. Keep things just as they are." He slapped Grady jovially on the back and strode away, letting the bird cage swing from his hand.

Grady surprised himself by hardly acknowledging the oddity of a man strolling through any town with a bird in a cage. Whatever had taken over Moraine was clearly infectious and he was coming down with it.

"Your neighbors don't seem to be any more progressive than you are," Grady said. He ushered Jennifer out of the way of a late-arriving hoop contestant who careered past them, pleased to have an excuse to wrap his arm more securely around her slender waist.

"We think we've built something very solid here. It's a good environment for the children."

"Speaking of children, where's Danny?"

"Nyla has him lining up for the hoop race, I imagine. That's where we're headed now."

About twenty youngsters of various shapes, sizes and ages were in position at the head of Main Street. They each clung to a wooden hoop, their energy and enthusiasm contagious as the crowd encouraged their favorites.

Grady saw a proud smile brighten Jennifer's face as she watched her son. With his own mother he'd often felt like a burden rather than someone to be cherished. Danny was a very lucky young man.

The race itself was something close to chaos. Hoops, Grady discovered, did not necessarily roll in a straight line.

Youngsters got tangled together. Two of them managed to swap hoops but kept on running.

Dust rose in a cloud to cover the skirts and pants of runners and rooters alike.

Grady found himself laughing and cheering with the rest of the crowd, and thoroughly delighted when every child received a gold medal on a blue ribbon to hang around his or her neck.

Danny ran to his mother to show off his medal. He received a hug and kiss in return.

Grady and the boy did a "high five" before the child raced off to the next event. He'd never before seen himself in the role of father, except in a rather nebulous way. The unexpected thought that being a dad would be as much fun as closing a big financial deal brought him up short.

Moraine had a strange way of changing a person's attitudes about life. Grady wasn't entirely sure he was ready for a full dose that would alter his ordered existence.

"That was a great race," Grady acknowledged, still pondering his doubts. He tipped his Stetson to the back of his head. "What memories those kids will have."

"Like the Fourth of July and Christmas all at once," Jennifer agreed. Her blue eyes glistened with an excitement that matched her son's, and Grady imagined she would look just like that when fully aroused.

"Did you have races like that when you were a kid?"

"Not really. When I grew up, Moraine was just another decaying mountain town. We started all the Founder's Day festivities about four years ago when we began the plans for restoration. I thought it'd be fun for the children to have a special day of their own."

Grady felt a glimmer of insight and made a sweeping gesture with his arm. "Was all of this your idea?"

"No one can do a thing like this all alone." She lifted her shoulders slightly and smiled. "But I suppose I have to confess, I was the original instigator. Then the idea caught on and well...there's just no end to what we can make of Moraine."

"I'd say you're a very creative lady, Ms. Sweetham. The Murdock Investment Company could use a clever person like you." Though she was the kind who led with her heart, Jennifer clearly had a good business head, too.

"You flatter me." Her smile was intoxicating. "But I'm really not very good at numbers, and I've never been particularly interested in stocks or heavy-duty investments."

Grady knew Jennifer had formed a special bond with Moraine that would be hard to break. The thought troubled him. He couldn't imagine Jennifer being happy stuck in an anonymous neighborhood while he was working twelve- and fourteen-hour days. She needed a guy who could love her full time. Anything less would drive her away—maybe into another man's arms.

A narrow-faced young man whose hairline was already receding came up beside Jennifer.

"Hi, Jenny, how's it going?" Wally VanPelten asked. His voice was deep and slightly unmodulated, as though it had recently changed, and his plaid shirt hung from narrow shoulders with as much pizzazz as it would from a coat hanger. He smiled eagerly.

"Just fine, Wally." She gave the young man an affectionate hug. "I didn't know you were back in town."

"I suspect my father would think it sacrilegious if the next president of Moraine Bank didn't show up for Founder's Day."

She chuckled in agreement and introduced Grady. "Grady came to Moraine on business and now he's agreed to fill in for Jake in the melodrama."

Wally straightened and his expression changed to one of considerable interest. "Murdock? Of Sierra Syndications?"

"That's right," Grady admitted.

"You know, it's a real pleasure to meet you. I did a rather super paper on your investment company. I'm a Harvard man. Murdock Investments is a terrific example of superior investment strategy over the long term. The sort of ruthless approach that means great returns for investors. It's in all the best texts. Terrific role model for all of us interested in the financial business." He puffed up his otherwise concave chest. "Got the top grade in the class, too, I'll have you know."

"Congratulations," Grady replied, amused at the young man's boast but not entirely pleased with his reference to *ruthless approach*. That sounded somehow like being one short step away from dishonest.

"If you'll excuse us, Wally," Jennifer inserted, "the lizard race is about to start and my son is sure his entry is going to win."

"Sure. No problem." Wally turned to Grady and offered his hand. "Maybe later we could get together for a beer. I'd really like to pick your brain about some investment strategies I've developed."

"With all the activities today and the show opening tonight, my schedule's pretty busy but I'll try to find some time this weekend." Grady enjoyed helping young people in their careers. And it looked like Wally was the sort who'd listen to advice.

Wally headed in the opposite direction, and once out of earshot, Grady said, "Nice young man."

"He's extremely intelligent. Took all of the academic honors when he graduated from high school. Captain of the debating team, academic decathlon, that sort of thing."

"Impressive. Sonora High's finest."

"He's also the only kid I know who's had his own stockbroker since about the age of twelve."

"The only trouble with Harvard grads is that they come out of school with some pretty wild ideas. It takes a while for experience to smooth out the rough edges."

"His father's sure Wally will make the most wonderful banker in the whole world."

"He might have some different ideas from his dad," Grady warned. "Harvard grads are pretty progressive."

"I'm sure they'll work it out."

They joined the crowd gathering around a circular rink for the lizard race. Jennifer felt Grady pressing close behind her to get a view of the corralled contestants, his breath a warm whisper across her cheek she couldn't escape. She was intimately aware of the breadth of his chest and the way his muscular arms had somehow managed to circle her waist.

He had an uncanny ability to tap into a part of her she hadn't known existed. When he held her like this she felt absorbed by his strength. He defined her, like the power of wind and water shapes the mountains, like the insistent surge of a spring-fed creek creates its own contours across the land.

She felt torn between the urge to flee and her desire to lean into his strength.

"As eager as Wally is for my advice, I think I'd rather spend my time with you," Grady whispered in her ear. "I'm still hoping for a chance to ravish you."

His nearness was hot and bewildering, his declaration so intimately paralyzing that her thought processes slowed to a near stop. "You'll be going back to San Francisco after the weekend."

"It's only a two-hour drive."

And a million miles removed from what she wanted, Jennifer thought. If only her heart would listen to her brain, it wouldn't be so terribly difficult to have Grady standing so close. She could smell the scent of morning coffee on his breath and wished she could taste it, too. Pulling her lower lip between her teeth, she fought the urge to turn in his arms and capture his mouth with hers.

A dozen overall-clad boys, plus a couple of girls who weren't squeamish about lizards, coaxed their racers into the center of a tin circle in the middle of the rink. Marty VanPelten, as mayor, had the honor of signaling the beginning of the race. He held the starting gun high above his head.

With the crack of the pistol, bedlam reigned.

Released from their enclosure, the lizards dashed off in all directions, padded feet churning, miniature dust clouds in their wakes.

Children shouted encouragement to their favorite contestants. Adults whistled and hooted. The tiny creatures appeared eager to win, or at least escape.

"Which one is Ralph?" Grady shouted over the noise.

"Number four!" Jennifer called back to him, pointing out a racer with a yellow numeral painted on his back. It looked like Ralph was leading the disorganized pack.

Jennifer smiled at the enthusiasm in Grady's voice when he yelled, "Go for it, Ralph! You got 'em beat!"

The chalked finish line startled Ralph and he veered off to the right.

Jennifer groaned in unison with Grady and watched Danny frantically waving his arms as if he could create enough wind to blow his lizard across the line. Ralph only needed to edge left for an inch or so and he'd be the winner.

In her excitement, she found herself squeezing Grady's hand, oddly aware of the calluses on his palm and the length and strength of his fingers, which returned a firm grip. Why would a man who probably spent much of his day at a computer terminal have calluses? she wondered for an instant just before lizard number seven scampered across the finish line to the cheers of the crowd.

She exhaled, hoping Danny wouldn't be too disappointed about losing the race, and tried to slip her hand from Grady's. He didn't release her. His gentle possessiveness sent a shiver of longing right to her heart.

"Should we go console the losers?" Grady asked. His voice played along her spine in the same way his thumb caressed her hand.

"You don't have to," she said too quickly. "I'll just find Danny and—"

"Hey, I had a vested interest in that race. If it hadn't been for me, Ralph would still be lost under the bank."

Jennifer found it impossible to argue with Grady. The feel of his hand on hers blocked the rational part of her mind. His circling thumb explored the dips and valleys of her palm, heating through layer after layer of flesh until curling heat slid up her arm and across her chest. The air weighed heavily around her; the sounds of the crowd drifted into the distance, leaving her acutely aware of the throbbing sensation between her thighs and the pulsing beat at her temple.

"Why do you have calluses?" she asked in a voice so quiet she was barely sure she had spoken.

"I'm in a rowing club. Eight-man shells. We have weekend races on the bay. And I play a little tennis."

Numbly she nodded her head. Grady was more athletic than she'd realized. He was probably in good enough shape to race her up to Blewetts Point . . . and win. She'd always been attracted to men with stamina and strength, to the way they could hold a woman and make her feel secure.

The crowd moved like a humming swarm of bees in the general direction of the saloon where the picnic baskets would be auctioned off by the mayor. Still holding her hand, Grady let the crowd take them where it would.

Jennifer mumbled some sort of excuse about having to help the mayor and slipped away before Grady could stop her. Among so many milling people, he immediately lost sight of her yellow parasol, then found himself standing next to Aunt Nyla.

"Guess we all know which basket you're goin' to bid on," she said with a self-satisfied smile and a twinkle in her eyes. Her print dress was covered with delicate rose flowers on a gray-blue background and sported a modest white collar edged in lace.

"Will I need my checkbook?" Grady asked. He was growing quite fond of Jennifer's aunt.

"Could be. Most of the men in town know Jennifer cooks pretty close to the best fried chicken around. Stuffed eggs, too, and an apple pie that's downright sinful."

"Sounds good to me. But how will I know which basket is hers?" Dozens of gaily decorated picnic baskets were spread out on a long, cloth-covered table. From where he stood, Grady couldn't see any identifying marks on the baskets.

"It's like the old days. The fellas aren't supposed to know which is which. Keeps 'em guessin'. Could be you'd make a mistake and bid up the price on my basket." Nyla's giggle sounded youthfully flirtatious. "My fried chicken isn't bad, either."

"I'm sure that's true, and I'd be delighted to have lunch with you, but could we maybe work out a deal? Negotiate an arrangement for a little insider information?"

Nyla lifted her glasses from their perch on top of her hair and settled them on her nose. She studied Grady in the same way an old-time schoolmarm would challenge a recalcitrant child.

"Just how honorable are your intentions, Grady Murdock?" she asked.

"Well, I..." He felt like a schoolboy who had just been caught sneaking a peek in the girl's locker room. Guilty as hell.

"That child of mine was hurt real bad once. I wouldn't want that to happen again."

"I can appreciate your concern." And maybe he'd better rethink just what he did have in mind. What did he want? he wondered, mentally gnawing at the question and finding himself unwilling to come up with an answer just yet. Just taking her to bed didn't seem like an adequate answer—and would probably get him run out of town.

Nyla peered at him a moment longer, her blue eyes magnified and made more intense by her glasses.

"Jennifer and her boy have a lot of love to give to the right man. If you think you might be that fella, you might want to bid on the basket with the lace bow that matches the frilly stuff on her parasol. If not . . . well, that basket with the pink rose painted on the side is guaranteed to have the best chicken around. I taught Jenny everything she knows 'bout cookin'."

"I'm tempted to bid on them both, Aunt Nyla."

His answer brought the smile he'd hoped for, and his guilty conscience eased considerably. He liked the role of hero much more than playing the part of a villain or a guilty schoolboy.

A few minutes later Grady's bid of fifty dollars brought a cheer from the crowd. Amused, he had the distinct impression the townspeople had conspired to jack up the price on Jennifer's basket. Most of the other lunches had gone for about ten bucks.

He handed over the money to Marty and claimed the wicker container. The aroma of fried chicken made his mouth water.

"You really paid too much," Jennifer said, meeting him at the edge of the boardwalk. "But in a way you'll get the money back. We put the proceeds from Founder's Day into paying off the mortgage."

"That wasn't why I bid on your basket, Jen," he explained softly.

"I know." She fingered the bow on the basket. Was his motive courtship? Or seduction? Was he the kind of man who pursued a woman out of habit? Or because it was an ego trip to make a conquest?

His lips curled into a confident smile. "Actually, I bid up your basket because Nyla claimed you make the best fried chicken in town and I'm starved. I didn't have any breakfast."

"What? She's always said hers was the best." Jennifer laughed in mock surprise, glad Grady had eased the tension that simmered between them.

"She was definitely my second choice. But if someone had outbid me on your lunch . . ." He shrugged.

Jennifer doubted he would have let that happen. He was a man who knew how to get what he wanted. For the moment it seemed to be her. "I did promise Danny he could eat lunch with me. He wants to go up the creek a little way and pan for gold. But if you'd rather, I can tell Danny to eat with Aunt Nyla."

"He's welcome to come with us. Danny's a nice kid." Grady gestured over his shoulder, indicating Marty VanPelten, who had a firm grip on Nyla's rose-covered basket. "Besides, it looks to me like Nyla's got her own beau."

She followed his gaze. "Nyla's been trying to catch Marty's eye since his wife died about ten years ago. He's not exactly a fast mover."

"That's never been my problem. Maybe I should give him a few lessons."

"I gather there've been a lot of women in your life?" she asked, letting her curiosity get the better of her.

"I'm thirty-two years old." Taking her elbow, he ushered her away from the crowd. "I guess you could say I've been around the block a few times. And I enjoy women."

"But no serious relationships?"

"Once," he replied tersely. "I proposed to a girl shortly after I graduated."

"She turned you down?" Hard to believe.

"Nope. She accepted, all right, including a ring that would have knocked your eyes out, but her idea of fun was to fly off to St. Moritz for a little skiing, or to the Riviera for a few days in the sun, all on a whim. She couldn't understand I had a business to run."

"So you broke it off?"

He halted abruptly in the middle of the street. "No way. She reappeared when it suited her, but it turned out she was seeing another guy on the side. He was an English lord with megabucks and a whole hell of a lot of spare time on his hands. When I found out about it . . . well, that's how my nose got broken."

"I'm sorry."

"Why? Because I got dumped? Or because I was dumb enough to fight for my girl's honor and then step in front of a very good right cross."

Jennifer realized his angry reply was Grady's way of covering the pain he'd felt. She wasn't the only one who had been misused by someone she'd loved. Knowing they shared a similar experience made him seem very human—and even more appealing. "Because she hurt you," she said simply.

His arm circled her waist. "It was a long time ago. No pain, no gain. I make it a point to put the past behind me. Haven't thought about her in years."

Maybe he hadn't thought of Madelyn in years, Grady acknowledged, but perhaps it had affected how he treated women.

He slanted Jennifer a glance, experiencing a sensation that came close to what a man would feel just as he slipped over the edge of a cliff.

Though he couldn't even give the feeling a name, he suddenly knew his life was about to change. He wasn't at all sure he was ready to take that big a risk.

Chapter Nine

She'd made a serious mistake.

Jennifer had never brought a man to see her secret retreat along the creek. It was like inviting Grady past the lock on her personal diary and made her feel extraordinarily exposed.

"Pretty country," Grady commented. He placed the picnic basket in the shade of an incense cedar where the scent of the tree mingled with the smell of fried chicken.

"When I was a kid I used to walk up the creek and sit here for hours," Jennifer recalled. She still came when she needed to be alone.

Fast-moving water bubbled over granite rocks and slid past a sandy bank. The opposite hillside was a profusion of purple lupine with red Indian paintbrush forming perfect exclamation marks every few feet.

Along the sunlit bank, the forest was an orchestra of soft music. Rushing water provided a sibilant undercurrent while a robinlike song carried the melody.

A nearby pileated woodpecker added staccato percussion notes and was joined by an angry squirrel pounding his paw on a tree trunk to warn of human invasion to his peaceful domain.

"I love the solitude," she admitted. "It's a very special place to me."

"I'm flattered you're willing to share it."

There was so much she would like to share with a man like Grady. Lofty lookout points with views to the distant valley. Shaded glens and the taste of wild asparagus and berries growing in season. Quiet winter nights around a fire. Marshmallows and hot chocolate. Love.

But Moraine was hardly the financial capital of the West. Grady was unlikely to view her tiny town with its clapboard buildings as the ideal location for an upscale investment company. He would never be satisfied for long with the simple pleasures she and her town had to offer.

"Mom, can I go pannin' for gold now?" The lost lizard race forgotten, Danny carried his shallow pan as though it were made of the same precious metal he hoped to find.

"Of course, sweetheart. Be careful you don't fall in the creek. The water's deeper than it looks."

Danny marched a few steps toward the water and then turned to look up at Grady. Hero worship glowed in his young eyes. Apparently a lizard-savior could do no wrong. "If you want, I can teach you how to find gold."

"Sounds good to me, tiger. What'll we do with all the gold we find?"

"Give it to Mom so's she can buy a new 'frigerator. Ours piddles all over the floor and she has to mop it up."

Embarrassed, Jennifer gave Danny a scolding look. "Grady isn't interested in our refrigerator problems, honey. You go shift a little sand and then come on back to eat your lunch."

Danny and Grady hunkered down by the creek, working the pan back and forth in the shallow water. Occasionally the sound of Danny's happy laughter drifted back to where Jennifer had spread out the checkered tablecloth on the ground.

Watching, she realized Danny was enjoying the special attentions of a man. In Moraine he had dozens of men who were good role models. But no one special. No father he could call his own.

The instincts that had sent her fleeing back to the safety and comfort of Moraine when she discovered she was pregnant had also protected her from further heartache.

Filled with an agitated energy that had no outlet, Jennifer stood and strolled to the quiet pool just past the sandy beach where her son searched for gold with Grady. Perching herself on a rock, she shucked off her dark shoes and stockings and hiked up her skirt. The icy water cooled her feet but not her anxious thoughts.

For a moment she watched the soaring flight of a rare bald eagle circling above the creek. Until Grady had arrived in town, her life had been as uncomplicated as that of a complacent bird in a pleasant cage. She'd cut her own wings. Now she was afraid to try flying again.

"Penny for your thoughts." Grady sat down on the rock beside her.

"I doubt they're worth that much." To disguise her emotional turmoil, Jennifer glanced back upstream to find Danny still hard at work panning for gold.

Grady remained companionably silent, leaving Jennifer intimately aware of his presence, imagining she could feel the warmth of his body bridging the gap between them. She wanted desperately to touch him, to explore his face—the strong lines of his jaw, the bend of his nose, the soft brush of his mustache.

In return she ached for the feel of his fingers combing through her hair, the touch of his lips at that sensitive spot just below her ear, the sensation of his callused hands traveling over her flesh.

With a sigh she closed her eyes and leaned back. Bracing her hands on the rock, she let the sun warm her face.

Slowly she became aware of the shifting of the current around her feet. It warmly kneaded the ball of her right foot, flexed her toes one by one, and then moved to cup her ankle with a callused hand.

Her eyes flew open. "Grady?"

"A little massage is the best thing in the world for tired feet," he said casually.

"My feet are fine." She tried to pull her leg away but he didn't release her. Instead she watched in stunned disbelief as he expertly worked the weariness from the delicate arch of her foot. His hands were several shades darker than her complexion, a contrast of porcelain white flesh against his ruddy color. "I have the feeling you've done this before."

"Just a little trick all us villains learn."

A seductive trick. Grady was full of those.

She gasped as his hand slipped up to her calf, working there with as much skill as he had on her foot.

"Feel good?" he asked.

"Wonderful." The word slid hoarsely up from her throat.

"I'm glad. Let's try the other one."

Fascinated by the erotic messages racing between her foot and leg, right to the pit of her stomach, Jennifer did as ordered.

Her left leg was fully as sensitive as her right. The stroke of his hand was slow and measured along her calf, conjuring sensations unbearably sensuous. She felt muscles deep within her pull taut.

"Feels good, doesn't it?" he said. "I like it, too. Very much. You're soft, Jen. Like silk." He continued to run his palm the length of her leg, each time slipping his hand a little higher until he reached her thigh.

She made a small sound of pleasure.

"Something wrong?"

"No. Nothing. I just think—" She couldn't think at all; only feeling seemed to matter. She closed her eyes and let the sensations wash over her.

She'd barely been aware how much she wanted the feeling of being cherished by a man—not just physically but in a far deeper way. She'd thought she had that with Danny's father. When she discovered how wrong she'd been, she'd carefully locked that hope in a tiny corner of her mind and firmly shut such dreams away. Effortlessly Grady had rediscovered them. The feelings were rushing through her like a creek forced into a narrow crevice between granite boulders.

Where would she find the willpower not to fall into the same trap again?

With a shudder she abruptly jumped up from the boulder and snatched her shoes from the ground.

"I thought you said you were hungry," she said curtly.

"There're different kinds of hunger," he observed with a sexy grin before her sharp retort registered. "What's the matter?"

"You probably ought to be working on your lines for the play tonight instead of gallivanting around looking for gold."

"In case you don't remember, rehearsal went beautifully last night. I'm blessed, or sometimes cursed, with a photographic memory."

She'd thought as much. It was probably one of the reasons he was so successful in his work. "Let's have lunch and get this over with." She hurried back to the picnic basket and busied herself spreading the food on the cloth.

Grady's forehead tightened into a frown. What on earth had gone wrong? One minute he was sitting there quietly trying to seduce her, and the next thing he knew she was throwing him a curve.

Hard woman to understand. She'd kept him off balance since the first day he'd arrived in Moraine.

He joined her next to the picnic basket. "Look, if I did or said something wrong we can talk—"

"Danny! Time for lunch, honey." She handed Grady a paper plate. "Help yourself. There's chicken, deviled eggs, potato salad, carrot sticks—"

"I'd rather talk about what's wrong than what's on the menu."

"Nothing's wrong." Clipping her words, she turned away to rummage in the picnic basket.

"Hey, Mom, look at the gold I gots!" Danny eagerly held up a clear pill bottle. Two little flakes of rock sparkled on the bottom.

"Good for you, sweetheart. You can put it with the rest of your hoard at home."

Distracted, Grady asked, "Is that really gold?" He took the bottle from Danny and slid the flakes from side to side, studying them skeptically.

"Do I gots 'nough for a 'frigerator, Mom?"

"Not yet, dear."

Danny plunked down at the edge of the tablecloth and snatched a chicken leg from a plastic container.

Handing the bottle back to the boy, Grady said, "After all these years, with the mines long since closed down, how could there be any gold left?"

"There's plenty of gold around but it's just not of an amount that can be mined commercially," Jennifer explained. She sat down diagonally opposite Grady, tucking her bare feet under her skirt. "The early mining operations left acres of tailings that are really pretty high-grade but would cost more to process than it'd be worth in today's market.''

Grady did some quick mental calculations about the rising price of gold over the last few months.

"That kind of situation could change if the price of gold continues to go up," he pointed out.

"I hope not." Jennifer placed a deviled egg and a chicken leg on her plate. "Any mining operation is terribly destructive to the environment and I've heard the tailings closest to Moraine have the highest gold content in the whole county."

Something ill-defined tugged at Grady's memory. A newspaper headline? A prospectus for venture capital? If his thoughts weren't so thoroughly focused on Jennifer and the way the sun highlighted her golden hair and danced across her delicate features, he knew he would be able to remember the thought her words had triggered.

She'd certainly turned distant and cold toward him. He could have been a total stranger, for all the interest she showed. He'd been relishing the feel of her delicate foot in his hand, and the artistic shape of her well-formed calf, planning just how he was going to make love to her. Then bingo. She'd rocketed away from him like she'd been burned.

Maybe, he mused, his fire had gotten too hot.

He couldn't very well force her into some answers with Danny sitting right there.

As soon as Grady finished his last bite of apple pie, Jennifer tautly announced she had to get back to town.

"I have a lot to do before the show tonight," she explained, hurriedly stuffing containers and trash into the picnic basket. She looked as nervous as an investor who expected the stock market to crash any minute. Maybe it was opening-night jitters, Grady thought.

"Aw, Mom, I wanta look for more gold," Danny whined.

"Another time. I have work to do," she replied tersely.

"Hey, tiger, how 'bout I carry you back to town on my back? Cowboy-style?"

Torn between the temptation to put on a temper display and his desire for a ride on Grady's back, Danny hesitated.

"You can wear my new cowboy hat," Grady offered.

A smile crept up the boy's face. " 'Kay."

Grady hefted the boy easily. He was a good kid— eager and bright. The kind of youngster a man would be proud to call his own, his son.

He wondered what kind of fool the boy's father had been to give up both Jennifer and such a super little kid. Grady wasn't about to broach the subject with her again. He'd known that first day when he'd stuck his foot in his mouth, Danny's father was a sensitive subject. He hoped she wasn't still carrying a torch for the guy.

He followed Jennifer along the path, conscious of Danny's slender arms clinging to him so tightly.

"Hey, Grady, you gots any childrens?"

"Nope."

The boy paused thoughtfully. "If you gets lonely, you could borrow me sometimes."

Grady's Adam's apple seemed to swell in his throat. "That's a very flattering offer."

"You could ask Mom. She'd let you."

"I just may do that. I may just do that very thing." He hadn't expected to feel so strongly about someone who hardly came up to his waist.

"Are you gonna come back to visit sometime?" the boy asked.

"Well, yeah, I guess maybe I could."

"I could take you fishin'."

"Afraid I don't know much about fishing, Danny."

"I could teach you. It wouldn't take much time."

Grady grinned. "I think I could manage that."

"When?"

The kid really knew how to put him on the spot. "Well, let's see. I figure with Jake all banged up, I need to come back next Friday for the melodrama." He thought for a minute. "How 'bout I show up at your place late-afternoon Thursday. We could spend a couple of hours fishing before dinner."

"You promise?"

"Sure I do."

Danny's little arms tightened around Grady's neck.

JENNIFER'S HAND shook as she applied her false eyelashes. The lighting had never been good in the basement dressing room of Moraine Theater. For years she'd been meaning to add another row of lights around the mirror.

Now she was glad she'd never gotten around to it. There were some things she didn't want to examine too closely, like the afternoon and her resolve to listen to her instincts.

A soft rapping sound on the open doorway caused Jennifer to look up.

She caught Grady's reflection in the mirror.

Villains had no right to be so damnably attractive, she thought with a wrenching sensation deep inside her. His black cloak only served to emphasize his midnight-dark hair and the way a lock drooped across his forehead. His tight shirt collar accented his corded neck. With a touch of makeup, the lines and planes of his face were even more masculine and his sensuous lips all the more inviting than in the bright light of day.

At some basic level he had a devastating effect on her. From the first moment she'd seen him she'd begun thinking about sweaty bodies and forbidden pleasures.

Tonight his eyes seemed deeply set and his gaze scanned her in an acutely masculine appraisal. She saw hot, liquid admiration in his dark eyes, and panic surged again.

"Are you all right?" he asked softly, slowly twirling his top hat in his hands. "You look pale."

"Opening-night butterflies," she lied.

"You'll do fine. The loveliest heroine I know."

"I'm not a heroine, Grady. I'm a flesh and blood woman who's made mistakes. Lots of them."

"You're also a passionate woman who is afraid to admit what she's feeling."

She didn't dare do that. "When are you going back to San Francisco?"

"I'm going to have to leave after the performance tomorrow night. I've got an early meeting on Monday morning that I can't change."

In a little more than twenty-four hours he'd be gone. Determinedly she ignored that thought and scooped up her bonnet, tying it beneath her chin. "Are you going to sell the mortgages to the other investment company?"

"I don't know, Jenny. I haven't figured out why they're offering such a huge premium. I don't like to do anything when I don't have all the facts, but I owe the investors a fair shot at a high return on their money."

"I understand." She stood and faced him squarely. "It's almost curtain time."

"After the show we need to talk."

"I'll be pretty tired. Perhaps another time."

"What's going on? Since the picnic you've acted like I'm really the villain. What's happening between us?"

"Nothing's happening."

"Look, I know we haven't known each other long—"

"What's the point, Grady? Your job, your life, is in San Francisco. After tomorrow night's performance we'll never see each other again."

Grady's scowl deepened. "So that's it? A few on-stage kisses, a little flirtation on the side, and poof." He snapped his fingers. "I vanish back into the twentieth century."

And she'd struggled to find a safe haven for herself and her son in another time and place. "That's where you belong."

"You bet I do. But I still deserve to know why you're so eager to see me go."

"Of course." She swallowed painfully. "You're right." She twisted the ribbons on her bonnet, forming circles and loops around her fingers. "I'm just not sure I can give you an answer that you'll understand."

"Try," he urged.

"You frighten me." The words came out in a rush.

He opened his mouth to respond but had trouble finding the right words. "I would never hurt you, Jen."

"Maybe it's not fear. Maybe it's just that you overwhelm me."

His lips tilted into a confident grin that did amazing things to her pulse rate. That's why she was so afraid of Grady. She'd vowed never to rely on those kinds of feelings again.

"I overwhelm you? That's why you're trying to get rid of me?" Grady persisted.

"It seems like the wisest course."

He arrowed her a look that made her knees go weak. "I'm not sure I'm following your reasoning. Let's see if you believe it yourself."

In a seductively swift motion, he linked his arm around her waist and brought his mouth down on hers. She fought the erotic pressure of his demanding kiss, and the way he cupped her buttocks and molded her inescapably against the nest of his hips. But her struggle lasted only a moment.

A throaty moan slipped past her lips, and his tongue penetrated her mouth in an exploration that mimicked a far more intimate act. Languid, wondrous strokes. Demanding a response. Conquering resistance.

His embrace crushed her breasts. The scent of his stage makeup and the sweet flavor of his mouth swirled through her senses.

Admitting defeat, she eagerly drank in his flavor, finding some small satisfaction in the low groan of matching desire that filled Grady's throat.

His relentless attack continued, moving from her mouth to the indentation at the base of her neck. She arched her neck to give him free access and trembled when he gently mouthed her flesh.

Vaguely she was aware of Nyla's footsteps and her aunt's announcement. "Curtain. One minute."

Grady grasped Jennifer's shoulders and took a step away from her. His eyes were dark with barely controlled passion.

"You're quite a challenge to a man like me, Jenny." His voice was low and raspy. "But you're probably right. We've taken this about as far as we ought to go."

She nodded numbly. He'd gotten her message. Just in time. Another moment in his arms and she never would have been able to say no again.

AFTER THE SHOW Jennifer fled the theater without taking time to remove her makeup. She had to get away. She needed the safety of Aunt Nyla's house and all that was familiar to her.

In her room she pulled off her false eyelashes, ripped the bow from her hair and applied cold cream to her face as if she could wipe away her memories as easily as makeup.

It didn't work.

Nyla burst into her room without knocking.

"Good heavens, child, that was the worst performance you've ever given," she said, her voice laced with concern. "What on earth was the matter?"

"The audience applauded. And they donated extra money for Jake. That's all that matters."

"Not in my book. Are you sick?"

"Of course not."

Studying her with a skeptical eye, Nyla pulled out a padded footstool. She sat down beside Jennifer. "It's something to do with Grady, isn't it?"

"What makes you think that?" Jennifer said, bluffing. She'd always hated her aunt's very effective inquisitions. The rack would have been easier to resist.

"Because onstage you treated him like he really is a villain. There were enough sparks snapping between you two to set the whole forest on fire." She sighed in a long-suffering way that matched her matronly black costume dress. "I thought you were gettin' along fine with that young man. What went wrong, child?"

"Nothing," she said tautly.

"Except maybe you've fallen in love and it scares you to death."

"No!" She couldn't admit that. "Besides, Grady doesn't want anything more to do with me."

"Unless I miss my guess," Nyla said, patting her hand, "you haven't given yourself and that man a chance. Why don't you try to patch it up?"

"It's not something that one of your greeting cards can fix, Aunt Nyla. Besides, it's too late now." He'd made his decision. At her urging, a small voice reminded.

"It's never too late till you're six feet under the ground." Nyla pursed her lips together and drew a deep sigh. "Just look at me. Never been married and I'm still tryin' to set my hooks into Marty." She kissed her niece gently. "I think maybe it's high time I told you my dark, little secret."

Jennifer smiled in spite of herself. "Come on, Nyla. There's never been anything dark about you."

"Ah, but you forget, lookin' at me now, that I was once young . . . and even a little bit pretty."

"Of course—"

"I met Adam McClure down in the valley. His folks were just plain ol' poor white trash and drunks. That's the very best you could say for 'em." She patted Jennifer's hand distractedly. "But Adam wasn't like that. He was ambitious and hardworking. No one would take my word for it that he was going to make something of himself."

"You fell in love with him?" Jennifer had always wondered why Nyla hadn't married.

"I loved him so much I was willing to go against my own parents' wishes. We were going to be married even though they didn't approve." Nyla stood and fussed with the lamp shade, her fingers trembling slightly.

"Something happened."

Nyla nodded. "Adam enlisted in the army. He thought . . . He wanted to learn a skill. So he could support me. We were going to wait to get married until after he finished boot camp." Her fingers stilled. "There was a terrible training accident."

"Oh, Nyla." Jennifer was on her feet, turning her aunt into her arms. "He didn't come back, did he?"

"Child, you get so few chances in this world." Nyla grasped her by the shoulders. "I lived with that regret for a long, long time. I should have married him. We shouldn't have waited one extra day. At the very least, we should have—" She brought her hand to her mouth. "Mercy, I shouldn't be tellin' you a thing like that. It's just that I don't want you to turn into an old woman like me just because you're afraid to love. And I'd bet my last set of bloomers that Grady's a good man. Give him a chance."

"I don't know."

"Well, you do what you have to do," Nyla said, kissing her and giving her one last hug before saying good-night. "Any problem can be solved if you just work at it a bit."

Grady wasn't the problem. Jennifer knew that. It was what he represented.

But in spite of her amazing revelation, Nyla was wrong. It was too late, Jennifer thought, glancing out her bedroom window in the direction of Grady's cabin. There were no lights on. He was already asleep.

Turning away from the window, she removed her contacts and placed them in their container. She stripped off her costume and searched for her nightgown in the closet.

She stared blankly at the cotton gown, wadding the sleeve into a ball and releasing it again. Going to bed would be a futile exercise, she realized. She'd never be able to sleep. Her mind was in too much turmoil.

Tossing her nightgown on the bed, she grabbed a pair of jeans and an old sweatshirt. She'd have a better chance of sleeping tonight if she got a little exercise. A walk in the cool night air might help her relax.

Chapter Ten

The wooden swing creaked under Grady's weight. After the performance, he'd only gotten as far as the porch of the small cabin where he was staying. He'd been sitting there for a long time, thinking and staring at the stars. In spite of his earlier statement about wanting to limit his relationship with Jennifer, he couldn't seem to decide what strategy to take next.

He'd make good on his commitment for the final weekend melodrama performance. Then he ought to pack his bags and get the hell away from Moraine. After all, Jennifer had told him to get lost.

Except she'd also said he overwhelmed her. No woman had told him that. Ever. And that intrigued him.

That kiss backstage had rocked him back on his heels. If he hadn't broken it off right then, he probably would have kidnapped her and worried later about the consequences.

So what should he do now? Grady wondered. He'd never before had problems dealing with women.

Truth was, they always came to him. Jennifer was a challenge—one that he was going to win. No matter what.

JENNIFER'S FOOT slipped on a bunch of dry pine needles. She held her breath, afraid to move for fear she would be detected.

She'd been watching Grady for the past several minutes, since she'd spotted him on the porch. She couldn't see much. The glow of his white shirt in the moonlight revealed his broad shoulders, his long, lean legs, his strong hands resting on his knees.

When she'd left her house she had intended to walk up the hill, not down to Grady's cabin. But she'd been irresistibly drawn here. Not to wake him, for she'd been sure he would be asleep inside. She'd just wanted to be near him.

"Is someone there?" Grady called into the darkness. The noise he'd heard had sounded unnaturally loud in the stillness and subtly human.

"It's me." From out of the shadows, Jennifer walked hesitantly toward him and paused at the porch steps.

The swing groaned when he stood. Slowly he walked down the steps and stood in front of her. With one finger, he lifted her chin.

A slice of moonlight glinted off Jennifer's hair. The way she was holding herself so tautly, he guessed tonight her eyes were filled with indecision. In contrast, he knew exactly what he wanted to do.

"Why are you here?" he asked.

She pursed her lips. "I was taking a walk."

He outlined her lips with his thumb, first one side, then the other, prolonging the sensation of flesh on flesh until he felt the sudden flow of her warm breath. "I think you were doing more than that, Jennifer. Tell me why you're here."

She shook her head. "I couldn't sleep."

He glided his hand along the ridge of her jaw. With his fingers he combed strands of silken hair away from her ear. He circled the delicate whorls with the flat of his hand and heard her low sound of pleasure. "You know the answer, Jenny. I want to hear you say it."

"Please, Grady..."

"You have to admit what you want. From me. For yourself. You're hot. Passionate. Don't lie to yourself."

"I want..." Her hands moved like excited butterflies across his chest. "I want you to... kiss me."

He played with her hair, lifting the heavy weight off her slender neck. He palmed the delicate column, kneading gently. "Yes, I'll kiss you. A thousand times. But you want more. Tell me what you want from me, Jennifer."

Warring indecision coursed through her entire body. "Hold me."

"Not good enough. Don't be afraid of me. Of us. Together."

"Dammit, Grady, do I have to spell it out for you?" As if the cork had finally released her bottled-up emotions, she wrapped her arms around him and buried her face against his chest. "I want to feel you close to me, Grady. Let me feel your heat."

His arms tightened around her. "That's what we both want."

Faced with an overwhelming need, Jennifer realized there'd never been a chance for her to win the battle with her conscience. Grady's heart pounded against her cheek, the beat strong and solid like the man himself. She felt a responding rhythm deep within her soul. She'd sensed that same matching sensation from the first, as though Grady were her other half, the half she'd been seeking for a very long time.

She lifted her face and his lips found hers, conquering them, claiming them as his own. Desire exploded within her. She drew in his flavor until the world shrank and spun around her. Barriers she'd erected long ago tumbled one after the other. She circled his neck, allowing her fingers the luxury of making deep paths through his thick hair. She felt ensnared by the sinuous filaments.

His mustache was soft and caressing; his lips firm and demanding. She inhaled breath from his lungs. It filled her and made her feel dizzy with the need for more, light-headed with desire.

His hand was at her waist, slipping upward beneath her sweatshirt until he palmed the curve of her breast. She gasped, the call of his name muffled in her throat. Exploring further, his thumb brushed across her nipple, turning it instantly into a hard nub of wanting.

Their tongues danced together, soaring, touching eagerly only to separate one more time.

Honeyed moisture flowed through her veins and she knew the desire she'd hidden from herself all these years had simply been lying dormant. Waiting for Grady.

"Do you feel it, sweetheart? How great we are together?"

"Yes," she whispered against his mouth. "I want more."

"I warn you. Once won't be enough."

"Who said it would be enough for me?"

Driven by an obsessive mix of physical hunger and enchantment, Grady scooped her up into his arms. He'd wanted her like this since that first moment he'd seen her and the stage had rocked beneath his feet. He was going to take all she was willing to give—and then make her give more until he burned with her hidden passion.

He raked his lips hard across her mouth, hungry and demanding, and thrust his tongue into her warm cavern. Her taste was of warm honey, her fragrance of a sun-dappled field. Fresh. Exhilarating. The anticipation of unspeakable pleasure arrowed through his body.

With the strength of a man possessed, he carried her into the cabin. Moonlight filtering in through the windows marked his path and gilded the untamed mane of her golden hair. Excitement radiated from her so bright it dazzled him.

Jennifer clung to him tightly as he released her legs and lowered her down the length of his body to stand near the edge of the bed. Unable to wait a moment longer, she worked with deft fingers at the buttons on Grady's shirt. She slid her palms beneath the parted fabric, across his broad chest furred with springy hair. She sought his nipple and suckled the nub. It seemed as though all of her life she had wanted to touch Grady this way.

A low, husky groan escaped Grady's throat. "God, woman, you're wonderful."

His strong hands at her waist steadied her over legs gone weak and nerveless. Some small inner voice warned her she was about to release an avalanche of passion—hers and his; she didn't know which was the most powerful.

She trembled when he lifted her shirt up along her ribs and then over her head, capturing her arms in the fleecy fabric for a moment while his mouth explored the flesh he had bared. Sparks seemed to dance like a thousand fireflies wherever his lips grazed her heated skin.

He caught her nipple, as she had trapped his, moistening the turgid mound through the sheer nylon of her bra. Her fingers clenched helplessly in the air. If only she could touch him again, dig her nails into broad shoulders, taste his salt once more.

"You taste so good, sweetheart," he whispered, mouthing her gently. "I'll take you over chocolate-walnut-cherry any day."

Her laughter lodged in her throat when he stripped the remaining sheer fabric away and tasted her more fully. Alternately, he suckled and nibbled with his teeth until Jennifer cried out with desire. His tongue explored the deep valley between her breasts. Her heart pounded so hard her whole body shook.

In the movements between them, she needed no script or stage directions. She played her role without benefit of rehearsal. Grady prompted her expertly with hands and mouth, and she followed his lead, ad-libbing with her fingertips to explore the long, hard landscape of his body.

Clothing dropped to the floor piece by piece, each article making a soft, sibilant sound as it landed.

"You're more beautiful than I'd even guessed," he whispered. His hands were his eyes in the darkness, grazing her flesh like a blind man might learn the shape of a beautiful sculpture. Admiration shaded his every touch.

Lifting her easily, he carried her the few remaining steps to the bed and lowered her gently. The thick quilt welcomed her, the cotton cold on her back, the heat of his breath pouring over her. She absorbed his musky, male scent until she filled her lungs with the erotic perfume.

Muscles and sinew leapt to her touch as she raked her fingernails down his broad back. She felt powerful, thirsting for release. She tasted his heat, gloried in it and demanded more.

In the darkness, his hand splayed across her stomach and inched lower past the blond triangle to spread her thighs.

"You're on a floating cloud, Jen. Do you feel it?"

She arched against him. She tried to speak, but all that came from her lips was a throaty whisper of his name. His fingers caressed her like a flaming torch, making it impossible to breathe. Hot liquid flowed from where his lips touched her throbbing pulse to the blaze he'd set afire with his hands.

"Jen. I want you. Now."

Grady dipped his finger into the fragrant scent of her. Hunger tightened his body until he let out a deep, soundless sigh. Jennifer's open sensuality made him ache with wanting. This desire for her had been there from the first, and now he would satisfy them both.

Her fingernails raked across his shoulders, scoring his back as though she needed to mark him as her own. He accepted her brand as he welcomed the velvet moisture that slicked the opening to her womb.

He visited her mouth once again, tasting deeply of her as his thumb circled her nub of pleasure. She trembled and drew a shaky breath from his lungs.

"You're ready, Jen."

His weight shifted on the bed and Jennifer almost cried in despair, but then he was next to her again, stroking her as he had before and kneeling between her legs. She threaded her fingers through the midnight thickness of his hair and heard him draw in a quick breath. An elemental need glittered within her like the licking of hot tongues.

Grady caressed her hips gently, the feel of her naked flesh like silken fire in his hands. He wanted this to be good for Jennifer. The best.

In the moonlight her breasts were cast in a silver glow, her body shadowed and spread in unguarded surrender. An emotion squeezed at Grady's heart, one he couldn't quite name. In that one instant of time he was racked by feelings of tenderness so urgent they twisted through his gut. This woman was his.

Slowly, he entered her. She yielded, moaning low in her throat and he felt her heat burn him with passion.

He claimed her mouth again, sucking her lower lip between his teeth, biting gently until with a soft cry she wrapped her legs around his waist, locking them hard, and drew him to her.

Lifting her hips with his hands, he thrust into her once, twice, again and yet again, more deeply each time until she cried out his name and he felt her hot sheath contract around him. He sped past the brink of a precipice higher than he'd ever before experienced and tumbled toward an abyss that welcomed him.

Drained, he collapsed, holding his weight above her on his elbows, his heart thundering in his chest.

"Spectacular," he whispered when he regained his breath. He nuzzled into the sweet-smelling crook of her neck.

"It appears acting is only one of your many talents," she conceded, a smile in her voice.

"Teamwork. That's what makes the difference."

"Hmm. Not quite like your rowing club, I trust."

He chuckled, kissed her softly and rolled onto his back. "Just as exhausting, but far more pleasant."

Jennifer turned onto her side and draped her arm across Grady's chest, feeling the still-rapid rise and fall of his breathing. *Pleasant* didn't begin to describe what she'd just experienced. *A fantasy come true* was closer to the mark.

She snuggled closer and slipped one leg over his. His thigh moved reflexively, and he muttered a soft, sleepy sound. She moved her leg slowly. The sensation of crisp hair rasping against her sensitive flesh sent a little ripple of pleasure up her spine. Grady was so thoroughly masculine it took her breath away.

With her hand she leisurely explored his chest, tracing the furred pattern from side to side and across his flat stomach. She eased her hand lower.

Grady caught her wrist. "What are you doing?"

"That should be obvious."

"I thought we just got done with all that."

"But, kind sir, you made me a promise."

"Promise?"

"You said once wouldn't be enough. I quite agree and intend to hold you to your word. As an honorable gentleman, of course."

"Now?"

Her tongue darted out to caress his nipple. "Whenever you feel up to the task," she teased.

Laughing, he brought her hand to his mouth and nibbled on the soft flesh of her palm. "Fortunately, my word is my honor so I shall endeavor to keep my promise. Forthwith."

With that Grady rolled her onto her back and pinned her hands above her head. Of all the sensual things he'd dreamed about Jennifer, he'd never imagined her as the aggressor. It pleased him enormously. That she would take such pleasure in their coming together stoked his need for her once again.

"You do understand the second time takes much longer," he warned.

"You underestimate yourself, kind sir. I sense you are already quite able to keep your word."

"Ah, yes, but you see, this time I plan to go very, very slowly."

She moved sensuously beneath him. "What a lovely idea."

STRUGGLING AGAINST the languorous feeling that weighted her limbs and pressed on her eyelids, she fought the intrusion of reality—which wouldn't be long in arriving if the digital clock on the nightstand was right.

With a sigh, she slipped out of bed.

"Hey, where are you going?" Grady asked, reaching for her hand.

"Home."

"Stay, Jenny." He pulled back a corner of the rumpled quilt in invitation. "Stay the night."

"The night's very close to being over," she pointed out. "Danny's a very early riser. So's Nyla. I'm not ready for a whole lot of questions yet." Not when she didn't know what the answers might be.

Picking through the clothing on the floor, she sorted out hers and dressed before she could change her mind. Already she wanted Grady again. Instant addiction, she suspected. Now that she'd let the genie of desire out of the bottle, she'd never be able to get enough of him.

Chapter Eleven

Jennifer broke off a bite of breakfast roll she'd bought at Henry Woo's bakery as she leaned on the boardwalk railing. Grady's black silk shirt with a few decorative white threads was definitely right for him, that and his hat shading his ebony eyes. Wickedly attractive.

And his tight-fitting jeans. Lord, his legs seemed to go on forever. Just standing still he managed to swagger. And her gaze was drawn repeatedly to the way his fly tugged across his groin, memories of the night colliding in her mind.

With a quick intake of air, she offered Grady a bite of roll.

He captured her hand and brought the breakfast roll to his lips. Mouthing her fingertips, he nibbled lightly, then slowly circled each of her fingers with his tongue. His moisture glided the length of the first digit and moved to the sensitive valley of the next. He repeated the process until Jennifer felt weak.

When sharp teeth bit into the pad of her palm, a heated knot coiled low in her body. She should have made Grady buy his own breakfast.

"If you don't stop that, Grady," she warned through clenched teeth, "I'm going to do something really embarrassing, like knock you down and ravish you right here in front of all these opening-day tourists."

He raised his eyebrows expectantly. "I trust that's a promise, Ms. Sweetham?"

"I reserve the right to change my mind." Not that she was likely to, she thought, finally pulling her hand away.

"I like the way you taste, sweetheart." His lips curled into one of those seductive smiles that made her heart thunder against her ribs. "Though last night you were even sweeter. My favorite flavor."

Sweet? *Wanton* was a more apt description and she'd loved every moment. She'd barely made it home before Nyla began to stir in the kitchen, giving her knowing looks and smug approval. Lord, she couldn't get away with a thing in this town, and Grady wasn't helping.

"You're supposed to be learning why Moraine is so special," she reminded him. "And why you wouldn't want to foreclose."

Grady lifted his hip, settling himself on the boardwalk railing. A guy could get used to living like this, he thought. He took a sip of coffee to go with the roll and enjoyed the sight of Jennifer, who had the look of a woman well satisfied. Damn, but he felt good, though his constant state of arousal provided a certain distracting ache. Jennifer, he admitted, still appeared to be nervous about the rather significant change in their relationship.

"So tell me what's going on," he suggested. *Besides the fact I want you in my bed again as quickly as possible.*

She took a deep breath. "Larry's working with a group of boys teaching them mumblety-peg. Playing around with two-bladed knives needs adult supervision. And, that group of youngsters..." She nodded across the way. "Danny and his friends are teaching them how to roll a hoop."

"Nothing much seems to be happening." Except he couldn't seem to keep his eyes off the tempting shape of Jenny's lips and the enticing swell of her breasts.

"Just wait a minute. You'll see."

If he had to wait too long he'd be forced to haul her back to the cabin, and the town would just have to do without their local heroine for the rest of the day. Although the thought of her ravishing him right here on the boardwalk did have a certain appeal.

Just in time a chunky boy of about ten burst out of the gaggle of youngsters, like a baby duck escaping its mother, and raced down the street to the cheers of his compatriots. The hoop wobbled but he kept it moving. Wheeling around, the boy urged the recalcitrant hoop back toward his friends.

A woman standing near Grady cheered. "That's wonderful, Bobby! You can do it!"

Grady glanced her direction. She was as chubby as her son, and beaming with equal enthusiasm.

"Do you know," the woman said, catching Grady's eye, "that at home I can't get Bobby away from the TV. He's afraid to try any sports because he's, well, a bit heavyset. It's inherited, you know. But here..." She looked across the street where her son had rejoined the crowd. "Somehow he doesn't mind so much. There's something magical about Moraine. This is the third year we've come up for opening day."

For a moment Grady watched the woman edge down the boardwalk, knowing she wanted to go hug her son, then he returned his attention to Jennifer.

"Changing the world one kid at a time?" he asked. He tipped his hat farther back on his head with his thumb.

"If I could have Bobby for a week, instead of one day a year, he'd be the skinniest boy on the block. And a darn good athlete, too."

"Maybe." He thoughtfully considered her idea. In a way, Moraine had been working its magic on Grady, too. Was it the fresh mountain air? The people? Or some bewitching combination he hadn't quite deciphered yet that made anything possible. Though he didn't have much of an urge to try rolling hoops. Something akin to a roll in the hay held far more interest. "The kids all seem to be having a good time."

"They always do. It's the over-anxious mothers like the one you just met who give us trouble."

Jennifer's blue- and white-striped gown had a lacy insert filling the scooped neckline and she wore an ivory broach on a chain around her neck. A row of tiny white buttons ran from the neckline to her slender waist. She looked good enough to eat. One delicious bite at a time.

"Why don't you make the parents wait outside the town?" Grady asked.

"Because part of the reason for this project is to bring more business and money into town." She gestured at his coffee cup. "Henry Woo's bakery grosses three times as much money during the summer now than it did before we began the restoration."

"I thought you didn't know anything about high finance."

She shrugged. "I understand how hard it is to raise kids and put food on the table when the county unemployment rate is well above twenty percent. We've probably doubled the per capita income in Moraine over the past three years. Of course, it was pretty low before that, and not everyone has benefited yet."

"An impressive accomplishment, Ms. Sweetham. You sure you wouldn't consider a job with Murdock Investments?" he teased.

Studying him seriously, she said, "It's an awfully long commute."

He caught her unspoken meaning. She didn't want to leave Moraine, and his career was in San Francisco. The thought disturbed him.

To cover his concern he cocked his head and grinned. "There's always call forwarding."

Her gaze slid away from his in painful acknowledgment that technology wouldn't solve their problem.

Damn, he thought. Things weren't falling in place like they should. In this kind of relationship he was definitely on uncharted ground.

His eye caught Wally VanPelten marching up the street with two men. The young man walked with a tilt at his narrow waist, as if his head was determined to reach its destination long before his feet. The middle-aged men with him were dressed in three-piece suits, their jackets slung over their shoulders and their ties loosened in the heat of the day.

Grady frowned. He recognized one of Wally's companions. Sid Rommerman was the San Francisco attorney who'd offered the premium on the Moraine mortgages.

He tapped Jennifer on the arm and gestured down the street.

"Do you know those two guys with Wally?" he asked.

She shook her head. "I don't think so. Why?"

"The distinguished looking gray-haired fellow fronts the syndicate that wants to pick up the mortgages."

"Why do you suppose he's here today?" she asked anxiously. "And what would Wally be doing with a man like that?"

Grady didn't know but figured he'd better find out and learn who the other man represented.

"Let's take a walk." He eased himself off the railing and placed his hand possessively at the small of Jennifer's back.

The touch of Grady's hand was like a warm jolt that skidded along Jennifer's spine. And she'd thought she was so relaxed and under control.

She'd been foolish to come looking for him this morning. He would be gone in just a few short hours. Her time would have been better spent helping Moose Pederson serve drinks in his saloon, while he applied himself to the needlework that was his trademark.

But as in the darkness, she'd been drawn to Grady's side. He was like a magnet. Her internal compass always managed to lead her in his direction. And, God help her, like forbidden fruit, she wanted Grady again.

Swallowing hard, she straightened her spine and shoved back thoughts of how lonely she'd be after Grady left. She couldn't dwell on the future. One moment at a time.

Wally beamed a welcoming smile, which Grady acknowledged with a nod, and then he extended his hand to Sid.

"Surprised to see you up here," he said. The attorney's handshake was firm, his smile a slash of perfect white teeth.

"I didn't think you got out of the city much yourself, Grady. And dressed as a cowboy? That's a change."

"Maybe we both should get away from the hustle and bustle once in a while. Does a man good." He'd certainly found an intriguing, passionate woman hiding away in the mountains. Though so far the experience hadn't been restful. Stimulating was a more accurate description.

Grady introduced Jennifer.

"It's a pleasure to meet you, Ms. Sweetham," Sid said smoothly. He held her hand just a beat too long. "Wally has mentioned your name but neglected to tell us how charming you are. Had he, surely we would have visited Moraine sooner."

"You flatter me, Mr. Rommerman." Jennifer withdrew her hand just before Grady's quick and unexpected surge of jealousy got the better of him.

"Not in the least, my dear." Turning to his friend, Sid said, "Allow me to introduce you both to my business associate, Dr. Igor Graeber."

"Doctor?" Grady asked. The second man was taller than Sid, with a hooked nose and cheeks that seemed to cave in above narrow jaws.

"Of chemistry, I'm afraid, not medicine."

"What brings you to Moraine?" Grady asked.

"The motherlode country has always intrigued me, Mr. Murdock. I've visited most of the old mining towns in the Sierras. When Sid was so kind as to invite me here..." His shrug was an awkward movement of bony shoulders. "How could I say no?"

Some sort of a bell tinkled in Grady's memory but he couldn't make any connection. "Mining is a hobby of yours?" he inquired, searching for the reason he tied Igor Graeber's name to a distasteful feeling. Maybe it was only because he didn't like or trust Sid. He was a slick manipulator, Grady was sure. The guy would con his own grandmother out of her funeral money.

"A hobby, yes. You could, perhaps, say that." Graeber's smile revealed tobacco-stained teeth.

Sid spoke up. "Hope you're about ready to accept our offer, Grady. My clients will write you a check whenever you give the go-ahead."

"I'm still doing my homework," Grady hedged. "I may want to up the ante unless you've decided to tell me what the proposal is all about."

"Put your offer in writing and we'll talk about it, young man," Sid replied. He ignored Grady's request for more information as he had from the start.

"Excuse me." Wally inserted himself into the conversation. "I promised these gentlemen a tour of Moraine. You know what they say about 'time is money.'"

Grady had learned that little homily at his father's knee, and learned the best investment of his time was careful research. "You going to give your friends a special lesson in mumblety-pegs?" he asked Wally.

Wally's youthful face flushed and he puffed himself up importantly. "No, sir. They've asked my advice about some financial matters. If you'll excuse us, sir." He gestured for the two men to follow him.

"What are they up to?" Jennifer asked when the men were out of sight.

"No good, would be my guess. They're an unlikely trio. Sid's always operated just barely within the law, if that, and I'd be willing to bet that 'doctor' is a charlatan." Grady tucked his hand into his pocket and jingled his coins. Damn but he missed the nice, smooth feel of his lucky piece. "But I can't figure why Wally would give them the time of day."

"When he was young he was always trying to organize the other kids into some grandiose plan. He wanted to be an entrepreneur but wouldn't settle for anything as simple as a lemonade stand. The kids would never go along with his schemes."

"Well, he's got himself a couple of very shady partners this time." He turned to Jennifer. "Could I use the phone at your house? I think I know, or have at least heard of that Graeber fellow, and I'd just as soon not use a public phone to check it out."

"Of course," Jennifer agreed easily. "Give me a minute to let Danny know where I'll be and ask someone to keep an eye on him." She didn't like the troubled expression on Grady's face. It gave her a queasy feeling in the pit of her stomach.

IN CONTRAST to Main Street, Nyla's tree-shaded house felt cool inside. The rooms were furnished in a modified early-American style that managed to tastefully combine a few actual antiques with more modern pieces. Colors were subdued but cheerful. The rooms created a solid sense of comfort and livability.

Grady thought of the glass and chrome the decorator had insisted were right for his condo overlooking the bay. Until now he'd agreed with her assessment.

Jennifer led him into the kitchen and pointed out a decorator phone.

"A Mickey Mouse phone?" he said. He eyed the instrument with amusement.

"Last year when we took Danny to Disneyland he insisted that's what he wanted for his birthday. Who am I to deny my son his fondest dream?"

"You mean you actually left the mountains and took your son to a decadent amusement park?"

"I confess. I love any kind of fantasy." Her laughter was as infectious as it had been on the day they met. "Besides, I'm not the old stick-in-the mud you might think. At least a couple of times a year I go to San Francisco with friends. We do some shopping, eat out somewhere special and usually go to a play or musical. We make a weekend of it."

"I wished I'd known. I could have impressed you with my season tickets. Fifth-row seats."

"I am impressed . . . and envious." She was also delighted they shared an interest in the theater that went beyond summer melodramas. "We usually sit in the balcony. I'm always afraid I'll topple down those steep steps and end up in the orchestra the hard way."

"Tell me when you're coming and I'll be there to catch you."

His words sent goosebumps shimmering up her spine. She imagined dropping into his arms and being carried off to some secluded spot where they could make love for an entire weekend, without any fears about what the future might bring. "You'd better make your call," she suggested hoarsely. She wanted so much more than a weekend tryst with Grady Murdock.

He placed his hat on the counter and fingered the telephone a moment. "This thing won't make me sound like a mouse, will it?" he asked with a gleam in his eyes. "I'm calling one of the men who works for me. I wouldn't want to shatter my type-A image."

"Don't tell him you're calling via Mickey Mouse. He'll never know the difference."

Grady waited until Jennifer had left the room before he dialed the phone. He wouldn't have cared if she'd stayed to listen, but he did have trouble concentrating when she was around. Images of her naked and beneath him kept interrupting his thoughts in a most insistent way.

"Hi, Pete," he greeted his assistant, mentally pushing the vision of Jennifer to the back of his mind.

"Hey, boss man, you having a good vacation? What's she like?"

"I called to talk about business, not my love life."

"You mean you're not scoring? Losing your touch, ol' man?"

There was a splash in the background followed by a feminine shriek. Grady imagined his assistant out by the pool, a bevy of young women surrounding him, as usual. Pete always credited every other man with the same sort of insatiable appetite he had for women, an incorrect assumption in Grady's case. He was definitely a selective guy. Though for the moment he couldn't seem to get his fill of Jennifer.

In spite of his one limitation, Pete managed to have one of the keenest minds in the investment business.

"Look, sport," Grady said, "put a towel over your eyes so you can concentrate on what I need."

Pete uttered a shocked expression.

"I've got to be in Sausalito early tomorrow, but I want you to check on a guy for me first thing in the morning."

"A guy?"

Grady told him about the doctor. "Unless I miss my guess, Graeber is a con man, and no more of a Ph.D. than I am. I'm pretty sure something has crossed my desk about him in the last six months but I can't seem to make a connection."

"Then that means you've gotten mixed up with some lady who's really getting under your skin. Not like you, boss."

"Knock it off, Romeo."

"Oh, the man is having a testosterone attack. You gotta do something about that, boss. It's unhealthy."

"Yeah. I know." Though his problems with Jennifer were far more complicated than simple male hormones at work. If that were true, he would have been thoroughly recovered after last night. Jennifer had to be the most passionate woman he'd ever met. She'd drained him dry. Or so he had thought until he'd seen her again.

"There's something else you ought to know, boss," Pete said, lowering his voice in a confidential way.

"What's that?"

"We got a couple of calls on Friday. Seems ol' Slick Sid has been making a few friendly calls to our Sierra Syndicate investors. They're a naive bunch and he's planted the idea they're all about to get somethin' for nothin'."

Grady's hand closed tightly around the phone. "What's he been saying?"

"Told 'em about the thirty-percent return on their investment he's offered. You could hear every one of 'em drooling with greed. They want to know why you haven't done anything."

"Yeah, well, hold them off till I get back to the office."

"I'll try, boss, but the animals are restless."

WHEN JENNIFER HEARD Grady hang up the phone, she returned to the kitchen. She hadn't been eavesdropping, but the sound of his deep, masculine voice had filled the house with a new dimension, so in contrast to higher pitched voices she usually heard. Grady's presence gave her home a sense of sturdiness and strength it normally lacked. His bass notes warmed her heart; his rumbling laughter made her feel secure.

She didn't want him to leave. Ever.

"Would you like something cold to drink?" she asked, noting the way his height and breadth filled the breakfast eating area. He was larger than life. Her own special hero.

"That's not what I had in mind."

The husky timbre of his voice pushed Jennifer's heart out of sync with her pulse. "I think there's a beer..."

He trapped her between his outstretched arms and the refrigerator. "Later."

She licked her dry lips. "Danny could come back any minute. And Nyla..."

"We'll lock the door. Where's your bedroom?"

"Bedroom?" Her voice caught.

"Take your pick. It's either there, or on the living room couch. Unless you'd really like to try the board-walk."

"I was just teasing."

"I'm not."

She risked the burning feel of him and placed her hands on his broad chest. "Grady, this is not a good idea."

"No second thoughts. It's too late now."

"You'll be gone in just a few hours." Gone from my life, she thought. "I'm going to call the casting office tomorrow. I'm sure they can find someone to play the part of Pierre."

"I'm coming back, Jen. Next weekend and the weekend after that. And what I have in mind, you can't get from a casting office."

"You'll get busy," she protested. "Moraine doesn't have much to offer a man like you."

"You're here." He caught her by the shoulders, his fingers pressing into her flesh. "I want you, Jen, just as much as you want me."

"We'll both recover—"

"I'm not so sure." His mouth captured hers as it had in the night.

She kissed him back with an urgency that surprised even Jennifer. He seemed to know intuitively how to touch her inner core, just what to say to make her mind reel. With Grady she had no defense. She could only hope he'd keep his promise to return.

He dragged his mouth away and pulled her hard against his chest, letting her feel the press of his arousal against her stomach. "Back to the original question. The bedroom or the couch?"

"Upstairs," she whispered. "I'll show you."

Sunlight swept the pink and green bedroom with dazzling brightness. All feminine, Grady thought, just like its occupant. Soft lines, warm curves and underlying passion—passion she was still afraid to admit to.

He led her by the hand and stood her in front of him where they could see their reflections in the antique mirror over a low dressing table. Wrapping his arms around her, he brushed his face against her cheek and inhaled the delicate violet scent of her perfume.

"I want you to see what a vibrant woman you really are," he said. "I never want you to deny it to yourself again. Or to me."

Jennifer watched their mirrored reflection in fascination as his fingers worked the buttons loose on her bodice, his hands so large yet expertly managing the tiny pearls. The dress fell open bit by bit, revealing first a bare expanse of her chest and then her thinly covered breasts. He kissed the crook of her neck. She shivered.

"Look at your eyes, Jenny. See how they sparkle."

"Yes. I see." And feel.... How she felt his breath flowing across the sensitive whorls of her ear and down along her cheek. He smelled of morning coffee and she wanted to taste his flavor one more time, but he wouldn't allow her to turn in his arms.

"Now watch what happens when I do this." His thumb and forefinger rubbed at the rosy areola plainly visible in the mirror. Her nipple went taut beneath his fingers. When he did the same to her other breast and then both at once, a low moan of pleasure escaped her throat.

She covered his hands with hers. "I'm not sure I can stand this. It's so—"

"All of your body responds to me that way. We were meant to be. It's right, the two of us."

He shifted and pressed the nest of his hips against the extraordinarily sensitive cleft between her hips, all the while continuing to work his black magic on her breasts. Raging desire shot through her lower body. She trembled and couldn't catch her breath. Her face was flushed, her lips parted, her eyes glittering back at her from the mirror, the picture of passion aroused.

Slowly, he slipped her dress from one shoulder. He mouthed the crook of her neck then glided his lips along her flesh, biting lightly as he went. She clenched her teeth against the cry that fought to escape from her throat and bared her neck more fully to his attack.

"This is how I see you, Jen, when we make love. Beautiful. Desirable. Passionate."

"It's you that does it to me. I'm not really—"

"Yes, you are. For me. Only me."

He slipped the second sleeve from her arm until the dress hung loosely at her waist. With a quick movement of his hands, her bra vanished from view.

"In the dark it isn't so—"

"Erotic," he finished for her since the word had lodged in her throat.

Even as he cupped her breasts, his hands tan against flesh that had never seen the sun, she was acutely aware of their weight and the aching sensation pulling at her nipples.

She leaned back against Grady, her legs no longer able to hold her upright.

He shifted a lock of her long hair from behind her shoulder and draped it across her breast. The filaments shimmered in the sunlight and teased at her flesh. "When we make love, this is how your hair feels across my chest, sweetheart."

"Oh, Grady."

"I love the feel of you. Your hair. Your skin. Your kisses. You make me hot. Hot for you."

"I don't want to watch anymore, Grady. I want you. All of you."

He turned her slowly in his arms.

Downstairs a door slammed shut.

Jennifer jumped as though she'd been burned. "Someone's home."

Grady swore.

Hurriedly Jennifer pulled up her dress. Unfulfilled passion made her body ache in frustration.

Grady made a perfunctory effort at smoothing his hair. "Damn lousy timing, I'd say."

"I'm sorry." More sorry than even he could imagine. "I have to see who's there."

"Right."

THEY DISCOVERED Nyla storming around her kitchen like a woman gone berserk. The mixer was on the counter surrounded by flour, eggs, a carton of milk, an array of canned fruit and assorted spices. Still mumbling to herself, Nyla measured flour into a metal cup, spilling half of it on the floor. The rest she poured into the mixing bowl.

Grady raised questioning eyebrows.

"Nyla, are you all right?" Jennifer asked. Bright dots of pink colored her aunt's cheeks.

"Of course I am. It's that fool man who's sick in the head." Another portion of flour went into the bowl.

"Man? What man?"

Nyla grabbed the container of sugar. "Marty. Who'd you think?"

Jennifer glanced at Grady. He shrugged.

"Marty has upset you for some reason?" Jennifer suggested, trying to understand what was the matter.

Whirling, Nyla planted one fist on her ample hip. "You're darn right he has. Can you imagine the man! He ate my chicken yesterday, nice as you please, and today he tells me he's going to take a cruise. A cruise, mind you, clear around the world. Maybe go for a year just because he thinks those fancy cruise ships have got the best food you can eat. I'll show him *fancy!*" She snatched up a can of peaches and jammed it under the electric can opener.

"You're making him something special," Jennifer concluded.

"You bet your little patootie I am." She cracked three eggs into the mixture. "The most gooey, sweetest dessert I can think of. I've got to save that man from himself."

Forget little things like cholesterol, Jennifer decided, watching her aunt drop a full pound of butter into the mixture. "Are you sure that's wise, Aunt Nyla?"

"It's the only way." She switched on the beaters. "Do you have any idea how many widows take cruises? The poor man wouldn't have a chance. One of 'em would have him hog-tied and married before he even made it to Catalina."

Jennifer stifled a smile. "Perhaps you have a point."

"Just wait till he tastes this concoction. It'll make him so sick—" she poured an entire box of powdered sugar into the bowl "—he'll never want to see *fancy* again. Plain home cookin' will do him just fine."

Grady whispered, "She's trying to poison him."

"No." Jennifer's sides ached with the effort not to laugh aloud. "I just think after ten years of waiting for Marty to notice her, she's getting a bit impatient. She's not willing to risk him to some shipboard romance."

Cupping the back of Jennifer's neck, Grady said, "Whatever she's up to, I think I'd better leave. This is no place for a man."

She turned, reaching up to brush his lips with a quick kiss. "You're probably right."

He picked up his flour-dusted hat from the counter by the phone. "When she settles down you might complain to her about her timing. We could have had—"

"I'll see you at the performance tonight."

"Count on it."

Chapter Twelve

"My child is an innocent, Pierre Le Evil," Marty insisted in the slurred voice of Rufus Goodhearted. Bent over at the waist, he staggered drunkenly across the stage, clutching his cane with a shaking hand. Grady thought he looked a little green around the edges and wondered if he'd indulged a bit too much in sweet desserts.

"I will protect her from you with my last breath!" Candice's father vowed.

"Which is likely to smell of whiskey, you old, drunken fool," Grady replied as Pierre, swirling his black cloak across his chest. "If you hadn't pickled yourself in alcohol you wouldn't have had to mortgage your home."

The audience booed, and Grady had to suppress a smile. Boos were at least as much fun as applause.

"You can't talk to my husband like that," Nyla cried. Her ample breasts jiggled as Merilee Goodhearted scurried across the stage to give her husband a bear hug. "He's a good man. He only drinks because he's in such pain. It's the terrible gout that bothers him so."

Pierre raised his eyebrows in disbelief.

"Get your paws off me, old woman," Rufus protested. He shoved her away. In an aside to the audience, he said, "Haven't been able to stand the sight of the ol' witch in years. What man wouldn't drink a drop now 'n' then . . . hic . . . if he had to be living with that?"

The audience hissed.

"Please, I beg of you," Candice pleaded, "give us more time to pay off the debt. I shall find employment. I swear I shall. I will work my fingers to the bone if only you will not foreclose on our poor, humble abode." She gestured broadly around the sparsely furnished stage.

"Never fear, my precocious pretty." Pierre waggled his eyebrows with evil intent, playing off another chorus of boos from the audience. "I would not want such delicate hands as yours to be roughened by menial tasks, for I have something much more . . . interesting in mind."

"And what is that, kind sir?"

Pierre leered at the innocent heroine and chuckled wickedly. He took her hands in his but turned his face to the audience to speak confidentially. "Little does she know that the railroad will soon offer to buy her wretched home. But I shall use the knowledge to make her mine and make my fortune at the same time." He laughed fiendishly.

While the audience loudly jeered him, Pierre brought Candice's hands to his lips for a kiss. Unseen by the audience, Grady winked at her and let his lips linger until she flushed. She was having as much trouble staying in character as he was. Her lips kept quivering into a smile that was sexy as hell. And he kept thinking about last night and having her in his arms.

He wished they were alone. He hated that he had to leave right after the performance.

Never in his life had he desired a woman the way he ached for Jennifer. He wanted to hold her, cherish her and kiss her senseless. If wishes could come true, the audience and cast would all magically vanish and leave him alone with Jennifer in his arms.

But that wasn't likely to happen. Not with two hundred people watching. And not when he had to get back to San Francisco to find out what Rommerman was up to.

Reluctantly he released her hands and forced his mind back to his lines. He hadn't realized what hard work acting could be.

By the final curtain, Jennifer's nerves were overloaded with sensuous messages. They snapped and crackled through her body like high-power lines downed by an electrical storm. Grady had teased and baited her with double meanings in every line he spoke, with the heated look in his eyes that turned her knees as weak as cooked noodles. It was the worst performance she'd ever given. The most titillating evening she'd ever spent.

"Darn you, Grady Murdock," she complained. They hurried down the stairs to the basement dressing rooms, the applause from their final curtain call fading as the audience prepared to leave. "You have a mean streak as long as from here to San Francisco."

"Me? Mean? And here I thought I'd convinced you to cast me as the hero."

"Not a chance." Perhaps in her heart but not onstage. "A dozen times I blew my lines. All because of you. And that kiss!"

"I was the epitome of self-restraint, sweet Candice," he said, mocking her with warm laughter. He entered her dressing room and closed the door behind him, dragging a chair from across the room to prop under the handle. "And I plan to correct that oversight right now."

Frowning, Jennifer untied her bonnet. "What are you doing?"

"You're always asking foolish questions."

With slow, measured strides he crossed the room. The lighting caught the determined glint in his eye. His makeup gave him the look of a villainous blackguard intent on ravishing her. Jennifer's breath caught in her lungs. Backing away, she grabbed the edge of the table to steady herself.

"Seems to me we were interrupted this afternoon at a very critical moment. I intend to begin just where we left off."

"Here?" The question stuck in her throat.

His hands cupped her face, palms heating her already-flushed cheeks. He gazed down at her for long moments, his breath caressing her subtly, like a summer breeze, his closeness making her feel desirable and achingly feminine.

"With any luck, Nyla won't try to break down the door." He lifted one corner of his lips. "You're mine, sweet lady. Don't even think about trying to get away."

The mock threat in his voice made her tremble. "I've never made love to a villain before. Much less tried it backstage."

"Then it'll be a new experience for us both."

"Grady, do you really think—"

"I think you're driving me crazy."

A mischievous and very frustrated urge tweaked her. "And I think, Mr. Murdock, that makes two of us."

His lips found the target of her mouth. He tasted and tested, drawing her out, insistently showing an urgency that matched her own.

Already on the brink, desire flared in Jennifer. Like a match touched to a summer-dry forest, the urge was swift and uncontrollable. An eager moan slipped from her throat. She pressed herself close to him, linking her hands around his neck to pull his mouth closer, deeper, to hers.

Her pulse throbbed at her vibrant core, sending tiny star bursts of pleasure to her heart.

Lifting her at the waist, Grady seated Jennifer on the dressing table. The row of lights framed her like a wonderful, old-fashioned picture, and the mirror reflected golden hair streaming down her back. His hands looked large and predatory splayed across her spine. Her ruffled skirt and petticoats billowed around him in a blue and white cloud when he stepped between her legs.

"Lord, I want you, woman."

"Whatever is taking you so long?" she taunted, a bit breathlessly.

Muttering a curse, he searched beneath the yards of fabric for the top of her bloomers, or whatever the hell they were called, frustration compounding his need. He found the elastic. Tugging, he slipped the undergarment down her legs, aware of her hands just as busy at his waist. He sighed into her mouth when she released his throbbing length. A moment later he'd pushed both his pants and underwear down around his knees. This was no time for finesse.

Ready at last, he raised her hips, lifting her away from the counter, and shoved into her hard and fast, exchanging his unbearable ache for exquisite pleasure within her moist sheath.

"Ah, sweetheart, you feel so good."

Jennifer gasped. Her perch precarious, she clung to his shoulders, rocking with him, crying out a little as she strained to pull him even closer, her legs wrapped tightly around his waist. This was a new wildness, a primal explosion that began at her very depths and traveled like a whirlwind to spin her out of control. She hung on, riding the currents, until a second shattering eruption, coming fast on the heels of the first, propelled her over the edge. In response, she heard Grady's low sound of exaltation and felt him spasm in release.

The stillness of the empty theater settled around her, eerily quiet. Their breathing slowly eased and seemed to echo against the subterranean walls. She rested her head on his shoulder, her fingers combing the damp hair that brushed the top of his collar.

"Wow. That was some performance, Pierre."

"We'll do an encore when I come back next weekend."

BY MONDAY AFTERNOON all of the puzzle pieces were spread out in front of Grady in the form of a glitzy, three-color, venture capital proposal Pete had retrieved from the files.

"Damn," Grady muttered, slapping the glossy cover closed. "It was all there in Moraine and I missed every single clue. I knew about the gold in the streams. I figured that there was a market for more tourist accommodations." He clenched his fists in frustration. "I even mentally compared a beaver pond to a spa and knew that Moraine kid, Wally, had done a report on Murdock Investments. But nothing connected!"

"Easy, boss," Pete drawled. He sat across the desk from Grady, slouched in one of the two plush velour chairs, his leg draped over one of the chromium arms. A heavy gold necklace with a medallion circled his neck and an earring dangled from his left ear. "You were in over your head 'cause of that fancy bit of fluff you met. When it comes to women, maybe you ought to let me handle the investigations. I'd be happy to check out Moraine for you. Just to see if you missed anything." A smile that was downright predatory crossed Pete's boyishly round face.

"Not on your life, buddy. The whole of Tuolumne County is definitely off limits to you. The girls wouldn't have a chance against your charms."

"Yeah, I know."

Grady chuckled and stared out the office window at the San Francisco skyline. He couldn't get Jennifer's charms out of his mind, and didn't have the vaguest idea what to do about it. She haunted him. Her face was everywhere. Even now he could recall her sweet violet scent. It seemed to cling to him, just as she had held on to him in the night. Better than good sex. No woman had ever given more of herself, moving him so deeply he wished he knew how to be as personally generous. That kind of giving was a part of her nature. He felt like he needed a remedial course.

"We still got problems with ol' Slick Sid, boss. Couple of more investors called this morning."

Grady brought his thoughts back to the future of Sierra Syndications and his clients' trust. Fingering the glossy folder, he did some mental calculations about his own net worth. There wouldn't be much of a cushion left but he could swing it. Maybe that was something else Jennifer had taught him. Bottom lines weren't all that important.

He leaned back, a little smile playing across his face. "Tell the investors I've got it covered."

His assistant raised his eyebrows in surprise.

After Pete left, Grady swiveled his chair to look up at his father's portrait on the walnut-paneled wall. He was a distinguished but dour-faced man with a hard look in his dark eyes. Murdock Investments was a monument to the man. Grady had helped keep the memory alive—an acknowledged philosophy of ruthless investments to balloon the bottom line. He was suddenly less sure how proud he should be of his contribution to that reputation.

Jennifer invested her heart, not dollars, in the things she cared about. Maybe it wasn't the most lucrative investment strategy but it worked. Almost magically, he decided.

Grady wondered what he still owed his father. The man hadn't cared a damn about his baseball home runs. Would he care that Grady had trebled Murdock Investments's net worth in the last ten years? Probably not. He had always been too busy cutting a deal for himself.

Rising from his chair, he paced across the room to look out the window. A summer haze hung over the familiar view of the city, blurring the stark outlines of skyscrapers and misting the bay. His whole life had been devoted to Murdock Investments. Changing that would be a wrenching experience.

JENNIFER STEPPED OUT onto the back porch where dusk cast deepening shadows. Four days since she'd seen Grady. In that brief a time, all of her sweet memories of making love with him and her half-formed plans for their future had turned to bitter reality.

Danny sat on a rock beside the house, just where he'd been waiting since noon. His spinning rod, like a lonely sentinel, leaned against a tree; his bait box sat next to it on the ground. Her son's baseball cap perched crookedly on his head. He looked so forlorn it nearly broke her heart. She hadn't known until her son informed her that he had a fishing date with Grady.

Damn you, Grady Murdock, for hurting my son.

"It's late, Danny," she said hoarsely. "Time to come inside."

"He's comin', Mom. He promised."

How could she have let her son get his hopes up so high? Mothers were supposed to protect their children from heartache. No chance for that, when she hadn't managed the same trick for herself. "Even if Grady came now, it's too dark to go fishing."

"He said he wanted to learn how to fish."

"I know, son." She knelt beside him. Danny's chin wobbled in spite of his hours-long battle against tears. "Sometimes grown-ups can't keep their promises, no matter how much they meant to at the time." A harsh reality she'd hoped Danny would never have to learn.

"I told Billy I was goin' fishin'."

"He'll understand." Though she would never understand how a grown man could break a promise to a child without so much as a phone call. She'd even tried to reach Grady at his San Francisco office but by that time his business was closed for the day.

"How about I make us some hot chocolate?" She rubbed the back of her fingers along the softness of

Danny's cheek. Hurts go so deep when you are only six. "Then you can pick out whatever bedtime story you'd like me to read."

"Just a few more minutes, Mom. Please."

His pleading voice tore her up. She wrapped him in her arms. As if a dyke had broken, tears came at last and his sturdy little body shook with silent sobs.

Lifting Danny as she had when he was a baby, she held his head at the crook of her neck and patted his back.

"It's all right to cry, honey. When you want something so much and you just can't have it, it's okay to cry."

Danny drew a shuddering breath. "I thought he liked me, Mom."

"Things happen, honey. Try not to let it hurt too much." *I thought he liked me, too.*

She carried him inside and eventually tucked her son in bed.

DANNY SEEMED just as dejected the next morning. He moped around the house, refusing to go and play with his friends. Jennifer didn't feel much better.

She forcefully set her emotions aside. No matter what Grady did or didn't do, she had the future of Moraine to think about. She wasn't going to let anyone destroy what she'd worked so hard to build—a good life with her son in a town she cared about.

The Mickey Mouse phone sat in the middle of the kitchen table. Her papers and notes were strewn all around.

Thoughtfully she tapped the pencil eraser to her teeth. "Nyla, does Millie know she's going to have to use Jake's truck to pick up the chickens? Those fryers are going to take up a lot of room and I'm not sure they'll all fit in her compact."

"Of course she knows, dear. You've had us all in such a dither for the past few days it's like you've organized assault troops for an invasion." Standing at the sink, Nyla was up to her elbows in potatoes and peelings. Two big pots boiled on the stove, making the temperature in the room uncomfortably warm. Sweat beads glistened on her forehead. "Fact is, Millie left hours ago for the valley. She wanted to get those birds back here in plenty of time for us to fry 'em up."

"I suppose I have been a terrible nag. I'm just afraid I'll leave out some detail and we'll lose our shirts. The object is to make money, lots of it."

"Everything will be fine. You'll see. And you'll likely calm down some when that young man arrives."

An angry flush crept up Jennifer's neck. If it weren't for the play, she'd just as soon Grady never showed his face in Moraine again. Maybe Jake could play Pierre with his leg in a cast.

"Now don't you go jumpin' to conclusions, child." Nyla gave her a motherly look. "Grady probably has a real good excuse for—"

"The only excuse I'd accept would be if he was unconscious in a hospital all night. Then maybe Danny would understand." And so would she.

"You can at least listen. That's only fair."

"Fair is not breaking a promise to my son. Anything else is a low-down, dirty, mean, hurtful—" Jennifer yanked off her glasses and swiped at her hot tears with the back of her hand. She was not going to cry. Not for Danny. And not for herself. It was her own damned fault she'd gotten herself in so deep. She wouldn't share that burden with her aunt.

The screen door squeaked open.

"He's here, Mom." Danny stood by the door in his cowboy outfit. "Grady's got a truck this time."

Jennifer drew a deep breath and her heart did a good imitation of a sledge hammer against her ribs. Standing, she walked slowly toward the door, forcing her face into a calm mask. Her pride wouldn't allow her to let Grady see how much she'd been hurt. He'd made no promises to her. Only to Danny.

She cupped her son's shoulder.

Whistling to himself, Grady hopped up into the back of the rental pickup truck. Bonbon, tail wagging furiously, leapt up beside him and a moment later Zorro perched himself on top of the cab.

"Hi, guys." Grady greeted Bonbon with a scratch behind one ear and pulled an apple out of his pocket, tossing the treat to Zorro. When he turned, he spotted Jennifer and Danny standing on the back porch. The smile froze on his face. It was like a January storm had just swept through Moraine leaving two tiny icebergs behind.

He cocked his head. Something was decidedly wrong. Maybe they didn't recognize him in his tattered jeans and old flannel shirt.

His gaze slid past Jennifer. With a sinking feeling, he spotted the fishing pole leaning against a tree.

He groaned inwardly and felt sick to his stomach. How could he have forgotten his fishing date with Danny?

Slowly he climbed out of the truck. "I guess I blew it, tiger. I'm sorry. I totally forgot about our fishing trip."

Jennifer's fingers squeezed her boy's shoulder more tightly.

"I told Billy you was comin'," Danny said. "I was gonna teach you how."

The hurt in the kid's eyes was as painful as if he'd sliced a knife across Grady's throat. "I got really busy. A lot of work had piled up since I was gone a couple of days last week. And we had this multimillion-dollar package we were putting together—"

The feeling of déjà vu slapped Grady in the face. He could actually see his father sitting behind his big oak desk. He remembered every broken promise—the baseball games his father never saw him play, the school plays he never attended, the graduation he missed—all because of some rotten million-dollar deal.

Just like my father. All the attributes Grady had vowed to avoid. Ruthless. Interested only in the bottom line. No time for the things in life that really count. Like keeping a promise to a little kid. A kid who deserved a whole lot better.

The shocking realization of how identically he'd grown into his father's image stunned Grady. He was nothing more than a clone of a dead man. He'd succeeded in becoming exactly the sort of man he'd resented all of his life. Not resented, he corrected himself. He'd loved his father with all the ferocity a kid could muster but it never seemed to be enough.

Congratulations, ol' buddy, for turning out to be the same kind of guy.

Grady knelt so he was eye-level with the boy. "The money deal could have waited. I'm so damn sorry, Danny. I forgot we were going fishing, but it was important to me. If I'd remembered I would have dropped everything—"

"You don't have to make up stories to appease your conscience," Jennifer warned tautly. "He understands your business is important—"

"No, it isn't," Grady insisted, anxious to make amends as quickly as possible. "In fact, how about we try our fishing luck right now?"

"Fish don't bite good in the middle of the day."

"They don't?"

"Nope." Danny stubbornly refused to give an inch.

"I didn't know that." He also didn't have a clue what he could say to gain the boy's forgiveness. Talk about feeling like a heel. "Tell you what, Danny. We'll make another date to go fishing only this time you can watch me write it right in my calendar book. I look at that calendar every single morning. If our date's there, I won't forget."

"Maybe."

A small concession. "I did bring you a present. You and your mom."

Reluctant interest sparked in the boy's blue eyes. "You did?"

"Yep. Look in the back of the truck."

The boy's eyes widened slightly, and a little smile crept up his cheeks. "A 'frigerator?" Awed, he tugged on the edge of his mother's cutoff shorts. "Do you see that, Mom? It's huuuge. Bigger even that Billy's 'frigerator."

"We can't accept that kind of gift from Grady." Jennifer was adamant.

"Aw, Mom."

Grady knew he had another fence to mend. Standing, he looked at Jennifer. It was the first time he'd seen her in broad daylight wearing her glasses.

In spite of himself, he grinned. "On you, glasses look sexy." Her eyes had never looked more appealing.

Self-consciously, Jennifer settled her glasses more firmly on her nose, gazing back at him with a stubborn lift to her chin. "I'm sorry but we simply can't accept such an expensive present from you. You'll have to take it back."

"Now you listen here, child," Aunt Nyla said sternly. She'd come to the back door and was looking longingly at the refrigerator. "If you can't see your way clear to accepting a gift from that young man sure as heck can. No way that boy is going to drive away from my house with that refrigerator still in his truck. Not if'n I have to haul it out of there myself.''

Thank heaven for Aunt Nyla, Grady thought. With a little luck, she could help smooth things over.

''I'd be honored if you would accept this small token of my affection, Aunt Nyla,'' Grady said with a mock sweep of his arm.

''I accept with sincere thanks,'' Nyla said, her eyes reminding him that a refrigerator didn't entirely make up for forgetting about Danny.

''Keeping your promise to Danny would have been a much nicer gift,'' Jennifer said under her breath. ''He was up at six in the morning to dig worms. He waited all day for you. I had to beg him to come inside when it got dark.''

Grady deserved her anger but it still hurt. ''I said I was sorry. I meant it.''

Her rigid silence was like an ice storm.

''I brought you another gift. I was going to give it to you when we were alone. But under the circumstances...'' He went to the truck and retrieved a white cardboard box from under the seat. The embossed seal of the most elegant store in San Francisco decorated the top.

He returned to Jennifer.

''Don't you understand?'' she said. ''I don't want anything from you. Nothing at all.''

A muscle rippled at her jaw. Grady desperately wanted to kiss her anger away.

"Just look, Jen," he pleaded. "That's all I ask."
And your forgiveness. "If you don't like it, I'll take it back."

A mixture of anger and curiosity etched her face. Very slowly she lifted the lid of the box.

Chapter Thirteen

A nightgown. Black. Lacy. So skimpy it probably wouldn't cover her—

Jennifer's gaze snapped up to Grady. Her whole body flushed. She thought of his hands caressing her, while she wore the gown, Grady holding her close to his body. The erotic image brought an instant response low in her belly.

But she'd be damned if she was going to admit it to him now. Thank goodness Nyla and Danny were examining the refrigerator and hadn't seen Grady's far more personal gift to her.

She stuffed the gown back into the box and squeezed the lid closed. "I can't accept—"

"I'm glad you like it. When I saw it I thought of you."

She wanted to wipe the cocky grin from his face. But dammit all, she liked what his smile did to her.

"You can't make up for what you've done to Danny by—"

"I didn't intend to." He wrapped his hands around hers on the box. His fingers were long and strong, and the memories of the erotic ways in which he had touched her sizzled from Jennifer's heart to her toes... and how she had responded so willingly. "In fact, when I bought that little piece of fluff, Danny was the farthest thing from my mind. And my intentions toward you were anything but honorable."

"Obviously." She torqued her jaw.

He tilted one side of his mouth into a wicked smile and lifted an eyebrow. "Aren't you glad?"

"No!" she lied in a harsh whisper. "Take it back."

"Not a chance, sweetheart. I want to see you wearing that tonight. For about thirty seconds. Then I have another idea. One I'm sure we'll both enjoy."

The arrogance of the man! The absolute gall! He assumed she would hop into bed with him simply because...

She squeezed so hard on the box that the sides folded.

"If'n we're goin' to get much use out of this refrigerator," Nyla called from the truck, "best we get it on inside."

"Be right with you, Aunt Nyla," Grady responded. He gave Jennifer a wink. "Maybe if I can control myself that nightie will last a full forty-five seconds, but don't count on it." He turned toward the truck.

Jennifer fumed at his back. The man even had the nerve to like her in glasses!

GETTING THE NEW refrigerator into place became a family affair, albeit reluctantly on Jennifer's part. Her emotions were too far on edge to be able to work comfortably with Grady in the same room. He looked daunting in his jeans and flannel shirt, like he belonged in her mountains.

Which he didn't, she reminded herself sternly.

And that nightie! Lord, she ought to burn it—before it burned her. She could almost feel the sinuous slip of the fabric across her flesh as Grady's hands explored every curve of her body. Her head throbbed as she tried to think of anything besides making love with Grady Murdock. Somehow he'd turned her into a raving nymphomaniac. A role that had far more appeal, at least where Grady was concerned, than she was willing to acknowledge.

Danny helped Nyla empty the old refrigerator, and Grady moved it outside, securing the door with a strap so no inquisitive child would innocently climb inside.

When Grady plugged in the new appliance, Nyla sighed with relief.

"Just in time, I'd say." Nyla peered inside at the wide shelves. "I've been worried sick how I was going to keep all that potato salad cold till tonight. This just about ought to do the trick."

"You're planning a party?" Grady asked as he took in the pile of potatoes still on the counter and those boiling on the stove.

"I had an idea after you left." Jennifer clipped her words angrily. "It came to me Sunday night." After he'd left for San Francisco and her head had been spinning with dreams that would never come true, while her body pulsated with memories of their wild, abandoned lovemaking. "We're turning Moraine Theater into a dinner theater."

"Dinner theater?" he echoed, leaning against the refrigerator.

The way he eyed Jennifer suggested he was thinking about that black nightie and just how she would look in it. He quirked his lips.

Dammit all, he was reading her mind. He knew she was thinking about the nightie, too.

She gritted her teeth. She would think about the town, not totally outrageous sleepwear.

"Nothing fancy, of course. Not like some of the elegant dinner theaters in San Francisco, but just right for Moraine." Though she wished it weren't true, it was suddenly very important to Jennifer that Grady approve of her idea. He was the one with good financial instincts. On the other hand, she wasn't totally unable to see a good opportunity when it presented itself. "We're going to serve fried chicken. Nyla gave the other women in town her recipe, and it'll be wonderful. Everyone's helping."

"It also probably means Marty will bid on somebody else's picnic basket at next year's Founder's Day," Nyla grumbled good-naturedly.

"There'll be mountains of potato salad and coleslaw," Jennifer continued, "and Henry Woo is making buttermilk biscuits by the hundreds. I made up flyers that we've had the kids distributing to every motel in the county to catch the tourists, plus we've posted them in grocery stores and anywhere else we could think of.''

"You have been busy since I left. Going to have chocolate-walnut-cherry ice cream for dessert? Second best flavor I know."

Grady grinned like a teacher whose student had just turned in an A paper. Or a man still bent on seduction. Jennifer wished his approval didn't mean so much to her. And that her heart wasn't doing fluttery little somersaults at the recurrent thought of him slowly removing her nightgown.

Valiantly she clung to her anger like a protective shield, ignoring his comment about the ice cream, which he clearly intended as another reminder of the intimacy they'd shared.

"If this works, by Labor Day we'll be all caught up on the mortgage payments and have money in the bank," she insisted. "The investors can wait that long, can't they?"

A troubled frown creased his forehead.

Hurriedly, before he could throw cold water on her idea, Jennifer said, "It will work, I'm sure it will."

"You're probably right. Depending upon how well you can control your costs, you ought to double or triple the theater's income. In fact, it's such a good idea, I wish I had suggested it myself. As I've said before, you are one clever lady."

His praise undermined her fury but his tone of voice was disturbing. "Then what's bothering you, Grady? Have I forgotten something?"

Walking thoughtfully to the kitchen counter, he began handing Nyla the food they had removed from the old refrigerator. "I've been pretty busy this week myself. You and the town of Moraine have some rather important decisions to make."

"What kind of decisions?" Anxiety crept under Jennifer's skin.

"About the future. Can you call an emergency meeting of the town council?"

"I can't but the mayor can."

Grady handed Nyla the last half gallon of milk. "I guess Marty is going to have to hear the story sooner or later but I don't think he's going to be entirely pleased. We'd better break the news to him first."

He sounded very serious. "I'll have to change clothes first," Jennifer said. "It'll only take me a minute."

"You look fine to me just as you are." His dark gaze traveled appreciatively up her tanned legs and settled on her halter top.

Jennifer felt a tremor of response and suppressed it. Damn his hide for making her feel that way.

"Town rules. We always have to be in costume when there are tourists around." She turned on her heel, marching to her bedroom, commanding her legs to do as she ordered. She would not think about how tenderly Grady had touched her, how his lips felt against hers, how much she had missed his uniquely masculine scent or how the cleft between her thighs had filled with moist wanting at the mere sight of him.

BY THE TIME Jennifer and Grady headed for Marty's office, Grady knew he had a lot of ground to make up.

"You're still angry," he said.

"No, I'm not angry."

He sighed. "That's a relief. I thought—"

"I'm furious. How could you do that to a little boy?"

"It slipped my mind. Things like that happen, you know. I got busy—"

She marched ahead of him along the path. Promises were made to be kept, not broken. Jennifer didn't want anything to do with a man who couldn't understand that. Not where she was concerned, or her son. In this case, she assured herself, she was not overreacting

He grabbed her by the arm, halting her in her tracks. She shrugged him off but didn't move away. No way was she going to back down.

"Give me a little slack, Jenny. If I could go back to yesterday and change everything, I would. But I can't do that."

"No, you can't." Any more than she could go back and relive the weekend she had succumbed to the temptation of Grady Murdock.

Hooking his thumbs in his pockets, he said, "I'm sorry I messed up with Danny. I'll try to make it up to him sometime. I guess I'm just not cut out for being a part of a family."

Jennifer met his gaze, her anger dissipating in the face of his sincerity. "What do you mean? Everyone is a part of a family."

"Yeah. Everybody has a mother and father, more or less, but that's not really having a family."

"Your parents—"

"Hey, they were okay, in their fashion. But they weren't exactly excited about a little kid running around the house. Not what you'd call real good role models."

Not excited about their own child? How incredibly sad anyone would have to admit that.

"Enough about me. I want to know if you're going to give up everything we had together because I made a mistake."

"Trust is important to me, Grady."

"Then I'll show you what you can trust."

In a lightning swift movement, he pulled her into his arms and crushed his mouth to hers. A hungry sound vibrated in his throat. Her seamless, hot kiss was more arousing than all of the memories that had haunted his dreams. Heat and need raked through him like claws of fire.

God, he'd missed the taste of her, her violet scent that drugged him, the pliant way her body molded against his in sweet abandon. He'd have that again. Every delectable moment to be repeated countless times and then it would never be enough.

He felt her tremble and finally submit to the passion that lit her internal fires, always so temptingly near the surface. He probed for her sweet taste and was rewarded with a soft sigh in his mouth. He savored the moment like no other before.

Framing her face with his hands, he gazed into the blueness of her eyes. Passion glittered there, as he knew it would.

"Grady?" His name was a hoarse whisper on her lips.

"Trust what you feel, Jenny."

"I want to."

He cleared his throat. However tempting the moment might be, he did have business to attend to. "I would like to dally longer with you, my precocious pretty, but I think we'd better go see Marty first." Then we can take care of more important matters.

"I'M NOT AT ALL SURE I fully understand what you're saying, Grady." Marty VanPelten's face had turned ashen and his ink-stained fingers shook as he closed the ledger on his desk.

"Your son evidently was researching a paper for school during the Easter break. Though I wasn't aware of it at the time, he visited our offices in San Francisco. We get a lot of students from Stanford and Berkeley doing their M.B.A.'s and we always try to cooperate. A Harvard student didn't seem that unusual. And except for proprietary information, we give them free access to a lot of our records."

Including venture capital requests from sham Ph.D.'s like Graeber, Jennifer thought with dismay. How could an intelligent young man fall into a trap that was such a blatantly dishonest scheme?

"Apparently he came across Dr. Graeber's proposal, which we had turned down," Grady continued. "Initially Graeber had tried to get permits and funding for an upscale spa resort in the Tahoe area. The idea was to appeal to the elderly, particularly those with arthritis, and would manage to separate them from their money as quickly as possible."

"Why older people?" Marty asked. "Why not anyone with a bank account?"

"I'm sure he'd take anyone's money and hoped the eighteen-hole golf course he'd planned, adjacent to the hotel, would draw a wider crowd. But his real claim, and what he figured was his best marketing device, was to tell gullible people that the natural water in the area contained enough gold to cure, or at least relieve, their aches and pains."

"But that's ridiculous," Jennifer objected. "Diverting the water would probably kill off all of the beavers in the area, and besides, why would anyone think sitting in a pool of mountain water would do anything for them except turn their fingers to prunes?" Or be such a sensual experience, she recalled, that she'd wanted the sensation to go on forever. Now that would be something worth marketing.

Grady turned sideways toward Jennifer and tapped his fingers rhythmically on the front edge of Marty's desk. His lack of patience seemed to be directed more at the scam than at Jennifer's question. He was leashed power. A man in charge.

"Actually there's a certain amount of logic to the idea, if not scientific proof," Grady explained. "It's the kind of magic elixir people search the world for and Graeber wrapped it up in a lot of quasi-scientific mumbo jumbo. His hook is that gold, in small doses, really is used in the treatment of severe arthritis. He simply lets it be known that he's a chemist, there's residual gold in the stream beds, and markets the whole thing to mailing lists of those over the age of sixty. Both Graeber and Rommerman are capable of making a story sound very convincing."

"But if Graeber couldn't get funding for the project or the necessary permits in Tahoe, what makes him think he could in Moraine?"

"The permits would be easier here," Grady explained. "This part of Stanislaus National Forest isn't considered environmentally sensitive, according to Charlie Wilson over at headquarters. For a user fee, the forest service would approve increased recreational development if there were no serious objections from the local residents."

"I'd object!" Jennifer insisted.

"You might not have a voice in the matter," Grady warned.

Marty nervously cleared his throat. "I think I know where Sid Rommerman has rounded up the bulk of the funds. When Wally turned twenty-one he came into an inheritance from his mother. She received the money from her parents years ago. Until recently, I managed the account. Conservatively, of course, but the capital had grown considerably. I wondered what he'd done with the money but he was very tight-lipped about it. I assumed he wanted to show me what a good money manager he could be."

"I'm not sure you can blame Wally for falling in with Rommerman. He is very smooth. My guess is that Wally, knowing the problems with paying off the mortgages, approached him about development in Moraine and Sid leapt at the idea. He probably figured Sierra Syndications would snap up the thirty-percent profit they offered and never give it a second thought. Then he'd foreclose."

"You mean Sid Rommerman would own half the town?" Jennifer gasped.

"That's what he had in mind."

"And do it using my son's money." Marty lowered his head as though the weight of shame was pushing him down. "Rommerman would be able to throw everyone out of their homes, or jack up the rents until they couldn't pay it anymore. Then he'd have us all by the short hairs and we wouldn't dare complain to the forest service people."

"That would be my guess," Grady agreed.

"But surely Wally could ask for his money back," Jennifer protested.

Grady shook his head. "I don't think Sid would have gone as far as he has unless he had the money sewn up contractually. Wally is probably stuck."

"And so is Moraine," Marty pointed out with a defeated sigh.

Jennifer refused to give up so easily. She jumped to her feet. "We can stop Rommerman. Sierra Syndications will get their money. All of it. Before Labor Day. You can promise them that, Grady." Determined, she planted her fists on her hips. Grady had said she could trust him. The reverse was equally true.

"Rommerman already put a move on me, Jenny. He let the investors know about the offer he'd made. It was a windfall none of them could resist. I had an obligation to the investors."

"You mean you sold out?"

A little smile played across his lips. "Not exactly. I bought out the investors at the same premium Rommerman offered. I'm now the sole holder of all the mortgages in Moraine."

Stunned, Jennifer sank back into her chair. He had the power to do just what Rommerman had originally intended. It was as if he'd just stabbed her in the back.

"Are you planning to foreclose?" she asked hoarsely.

"No. I think this town is a good investment."

She did a rough calculation in her head. "You paid an enormous amount of money. How can you... There's no way we'll ever be able to pay all of that back."

He shrugged off her concern. "You and the townspeople have a much more serious subject to consider."

"I can't imagine what."

"Rommerman and Graeber want to continue with the development. A hundred-room hotel, natural pools diverted from the streams around here and a golf course the other side of town. They've got enough backing and have already begun preliminary plans."

"We won't stand for it!"

He took her hand, gently stroking her fingers. "Are you so sure, Jen?" he asked in an intimate tone. "You told me yourself the unemployment in the county is twenty percent. This project would mean jobs, lots of them. And plenty of business for the town, at least in the short term. While it may be a scam in many ways, Graeber's idea is going to make money. Are you confident people like Jake and Larry and Henry Woo wouldn't want a piece of the action?"

Jennifer's heart sank. Grady had always maintained he had an intuitive sense about good investments. She didn't doubt him.

But what would that do to her town? And to what they'd found together? Their relationship was still so tentative, any disruption could all too easily mark its end.

"As I recall, Grady," Marty said, "the mortgages the town council signed contained a rather unusual clause."

Grady pursed his lips. "It was the standard contract we've used for real property for the last several years."

"Including the escalation clause?"

"That's simply a protection for the investors so they get a fair return if property values go up appreciably. They share the risks so they should get part of the return."

"I'm not following you," Jennifer said.

"It means, my dear, that Grady Murdock, holder of the mortgages, will get a very substantial return on his investment if Rommerman's development takes place and the appraised value of our properties goes up over the course of the mortgage term.''

Her eyes widened in disbelief. Grady had a vested interest in turning her whole life upside down. In spite of what he'd said, he still could foreclose. Or he could do everything in his power to help the development along.

Either way, the bottom line for Grady Murdock would be a profit.

Chapter Fourteen

"It ain't easy to support a family around here," Jake said. Emotion cracked his voice. He sat with his leg propped on a folding chair, his crutches lying on the floor of Moraine Theater.

"I got three kids 'n' they can go through a thirty-dollar pair of sneakers faster than a whipsaw through a sequoia. Now that I got my leg all banged up, I don't know that I'll be able to work steady." He scratched his leg along the top of the cast. "Seems to me a hotel would have a spot just right for a handyman like me. I gotta think about my wife and kids."

"We know it hasn't been easy for you and Millie the last few years," Marty said, his tone subdued and worried. He sat along with the other members of the town council behind a table onstage. The furniture for the play had been temporarily pushed out of the way. Along one wall of the theater, tables that would be used to serve dinner were stacked in even rows.

Marty nodded toward a woman who wanted to speak.

"My husband does logging when he can, but that job only lasts a few months out of the year. There just isn't that much timber to cut in Tuolumne County, particularly with all the federal regulations about spotted owls," she explained. She was a young, angular woman with a smile that showed far too many teeth. "The rest of the time he works down in the valley and I only see him on weekends. Truth is . . ." She flushed a bright hue. "We're trying to have a baby, and I guess I'd vote for almost anything that would keep him home all the time."

A sympathetic titter rippled through the theater.

Rising from his spot in the third row, the local minister spoke. "I know many of you are not members of my congregation. I also appreciate how difficult it is to make a living in the mountains. But I would like to remind you that, as Mr. Murdock explained the situation to us, the proposed development is based on a sham. It's dishonest for us to take money from people who think they're going to be cured of something as terribly debilitating as arthritis when that simply isn't true."

There were a few murmured agreements.

Grady watched the ebb and flow around the room. He hadn't realized the full extent of Moraine. Nearly a hundred people filled the rows of theater benches, an unusually large crowd for the middle of the day. Beyond the restored area there had to be dozens of homes nestled in secluded spots he hadn't even noticed. A vibrant community that was now split right down the middle over development. A troubling realization.

Arguments were calm, but deeply felt. One thing about Moraine, no one was hesitant to speak their feelings. Never once was a person criticized or berated for disagreeing with his neighbor.

Listening to the give and take, Grady began to get a glimmer of what Moraine was all about. He understood why Jennifer loved her town and didn't want it to change. It wasn't the hundred-year-old facade that made this spot feel so welcoming. It was the people and how much they cared about one another that made the difference. That was the infectious magic that had affected him from the first moment he set foot in town. Their love was given unstintingly; it had a texture and warmth Grady could feel but wasn't a part of.

He felt a stab of envy. The residents of Moraine cast a glaring light on what he'd been missing all of his life.

When everyone in the audience had had a chance to express his or her views, Marty turned to the town council members.

Jennifer directed a question to Grady. Her forehead was scrolled into an enormously worried expression that tugged at his heart. She had a greater capacity for love and caring than any person he'd ever known. He wanted a piece of that love for himself.

"Just how large an impact would you expect this development to have on Moraine?" Jennifer asked. "Both in terms of jobs and the effect on how we live?"

From his place at the back of the theater, Grady stood. "During the construction phase it would be pretty disruptive. You could expect lots of heavy equipment moving on the highway, which would create both noise and dust. On the up side, employment would be at its peak then. Several hundred construction workers, I imagine. That would last six months to a year."

"I could use six months of steady work," Jake pointed out.

"Most of the workers would be outsiders," said Smitty Guterra, the costumed miner who had parked his caged canary on the bench next to him. "Where would they stay? Those construction gangs can be a pretty rough crowd. Sure, maybe they'd spend their paychecks in Moraine, but they could jes' as easy break up the place."

"Including my saloon," Moose, the owner, said nervously. He fidgeted with a skein of yarn in his hands as though he could find a needlework solution to the knotty problem.

"What about when the project is completed?" Jennifer asked.

"Things would certainly quiet down," Grady replied, thoughtfully measuring his answer. He felt the weight of responsibility on his shoulders not to mislead the townspeople. "If Rommerman is able to attract the wealthy, elderly crowd he wants, they'd probably stick pretty close to the hotel and golf course."

"That wouldn't bring in much business to my mercantile," Jack said.

"You couldn't expect the hotel to have a whole lot of high-paying jobs, either, though some people would certainly benefit," Grady continued. "The tourist industry in general, and Rommerman in particular, tend to employ most of their staff at minimum wage. People like maids, waiters, cooks and maintenance personnel."

"Shoot, that wouldn't do me any good," Jake grumbled.

"Are you saying, Grady, that the project wouldn't help our unemployment problem?" Jennifer asked.

"There'd be some positive impact on the local economy, I'm sure, but it's difficult to project just how much. Property values and rental costs would probably increase. There'd be some increase in sales tax revenues but that would be pretty well offset by higher costs of schools and roads. In terms of employment..." He shook his head. "Unless you people are willing to work for very little money there won't be a gain. And if you don't take the jobs, the promoters will probably bus in workers from down in the valley."

"People that wouldn't give a fig about Moraine," someone said.

Nyla stood and squinted through her glasses at her friends and neighbors. "Seems to me there's more minuses than pluses in this whole thing, but I don't see how we could stop the hotel if this Rommerman fella is set on doin' it. And we still haven't solved Jake's problem about havin' steady work."

In unison, everyone turned to Grady. He felt uncomfortable advising a town when he was as much of an outsider as Rommerman. For once in his life he wanted to be more than just an advisor; he wanted to feel like he belonged.

Automatically he shoved his hand in his pocket, searching for the reassuring feel of his silver dollar. This time, he was on his own.

Jennifer gnawed on the tip of her pencil, willing Grady to come up with a solution to the dual problem. He had the expertise and experience that the rest of them lacked. It was the perfect opportunity for him to show he cared about the town that was so important to her. If he could only set his profit margin aside, then he could earn back a part of her trust.

"I think you should know I have a financial interest in having Moraine grow," he confessed. "That's a conflict, and I may not be the right person to advise you."

An aching sense of loneliness swept through Jennifer.

"On the other hand," Grady continued, "if you are all in agreement that the hotel development is wrong for the town, and you feel you can trust me, I do have an idea that might convince Rommerman not to start the project."

Her head snapped up. "But that would cost you money."

He shrugged and cocked his head with an irresistible grin. "Yeah, I suppose it would, except there are some pretty clever people in this town who could figure out how to make it prosper by building on what's already been started. I figure in the long run I'll come out okay." His confident gaze focused on Jennifer, and she felt a rush of heat arrow through her body.

The audience buzzed their approval of Grady's comment.

Jennifer's heart filled with hope and she blinked back unexpected tears. Grady was going to help. He did care.

Marty gaveled for quiet. "I think we'd all be able to make a pretty strong case for an adverse environmental impact report when Rommerman requests his permits from the forest service."

"That'd have to be your last-ditch stand," Grady said. "The best way to win a horse race, I've always found, is not to let any other horse get away from the gate."

"But if he . . . and with my son's money—"

The rustling of a new arrival at the back of the theater drew Marty's attention.

"My money isn't important, Dad." Wally walked slowly down the side aisle, his expression dejected and his hands stuffed in his trouser pockets. "I really thought the development would mean something good for Moraine. But I've been standing just outside the door in back listening to Mr. Murdock and all of you explaining how you feel. It just never occurred to me Rommerman would lie."

The young man stopped near the front of the stage, as though waiting to be stoned by an angry crowd, and Jennifer's heart went out to Wally.

In the audience, people shuffled their feet and cleared their throats self-consciously.

"I guess I owe everybody an apology," Wally continued. He made a courageous effort to hold up his head with what little pride he had left. "There's no way I can get my money back, but I don't want anyone else to be hurt. I'll do whatever you ask of me, Mr. Murdock, if it will help the town."

"You've learned an expensive lesson about smooth-talking con men, Wally," Grady said, "but I've been known to do a bit of scheming myself. Think you're up to a little acting job?"

Wally beamed with the hope of redemption. "I'll sure give it a try."

"I want you to call Rommerman. Tell him I'm ready to make the deal." Grady glanced at his watch. "Say I'll meet him at the saloon at four o'clock."

"What do you have in mind?" Jennifer asked.

"Something that's going to take everybody's co-operation."

WITH ONLY MINUTES to spare, Jennifer hurried into the saloon. She placed the latest copy of Moraine's weekly paper on the table in front of Grady. He looked like the villain incarnate in his black silk shirt and hat, and so incredibly handsome she felt something tight and aching squeeze against her heart.

"Maury, the typesetter, says you have to be careful," she said breathlessly. "The ink's still wet."

"I certainly wouldn't want Rommerman to get his hands dirty." Grady quickly scanned the headline and the lead article. He nodded in approval. "Did you give a copy to Jake?"

"He has one, and I put four copies in the vending machine out front. Just in case Rommerman gets suspicious and tries to check."

"Clever girl."

He covered her shaking hands with his, giving her a confidence she sorely lacked. There was a dynamic, take-charge quality to the man that everyone could sense and that Jennifer couldn't resist.

"It's going to be all right, Jenny. If there's one thing I've learned over the years, people want to believe what they see in print. And a con artist believes everyone else is out to get him first. All we have to do is play to his weakness."

"I hope you're right."

"Is Jake all set?"

"He claims it'll be the best performance of his life, though he's still worried about his family."

"We'll take care of that later. How 'bout Marty?"

"He'll be here on cue. With his prop cane from the melodrama."

"Anybody ever tell you you'd be a great movie director? Maybe you ought to give Hollywood a try." Grady leaned across the round table to give her a deep, hungry kiss. A very public kiss that electrified clear down to her toes.

She took a startled step back. "I'll pass on the movie bit, thanks. I just hope this scheme of yours works."

"Work? Honey, remember me? I'm the guy with gut instincts that never fail. If everyone plays his part, it'll be like Rommerman wrote the script himself."

He glanced at the paper again, then carefully put it into his briefcase, leaving one corner sticking out. He placed the case strategically on the floor next to his chair.

"You better get out of here," he said. "Rommerman could show up anytime."

"But I want to stay," Jennifer protested.

"I don't want you to give away our little game."

"Grady Murdock, I'm the best actor in town and you know it. I'm not going to give away anything, not where that sleazy creep Rommerman is concerned." She planted her fists on her hips. "I'll bartend. What'll you have?"

With a grin Grady relented. "A sweet smile, darlin', and something on tap."

He directed an affectionate swat toward her bottom and she scooted out of range, protesting as she went behind the bar. She wanted desperately to trust Grady and hoped she hadn't misjudged him again. He seemed to be trying so hard to help Moraine. She had to appreciate his effort, however hesitant she might feel on a personal basis.

After she delivered the beer to Grady, she found an apron to cover her blue muslin dress and busied herself behind the bar with a wiping cloth. The mahogany counter was already spotless and the chrome spigots gleamed.

Moose, the owner of the saloon, had perched his two-hundred-and-fifty pound, football-tackle body on a sturdy stool on the opposite side of the bar, thoroughly engrossed in the latest needlework magazine.

Framed samples of his work decorated the paneled walls.

Jennifer jumped when the saloon doors swung open.

Looking flushed from the heat, Rommerman paused a moment to adjust his eyes to the subdued light and then sauntered confidently toward the table against the wall. Grady directed Sid to a seat with a good view of the bar.

The two men shook hands. Jennifer strained to hear their conversation.

"Understand you're finally ready to talk business," Rommerman began.

Grady took a leisurely sip of beer and signaled Jennifer to bring the same for Rommerman. "Young Wally persuaded me."

"He's a nice kid. He'll go far."

"Crackerjack fellow."

Just the kind of a naive boy that a con man would see as a ready-made sucker, Jennifer thought.

After she delivered the beer, Rommerman casually retrieved some papers from his leather briefcase. Not a one of the white hairs on his head was out of place. His cool acceptance of victory gnawed at Jennifer like a dog working an old bone.

"I took the liberty of having these contracts prepared," Sid said. He placed the papers in front of Grady. "You'll need to get all of your investors to sign—"

"Nope. I already bought them out."

Rommerman's plastic smile froze on his face.

"You'll have to deal with me, Sid, if you want to control the town."

"You don't miss a trick, do you?"

"As I say, I like to do my homework." Grady casually stretched out his long legs and crossed his booted ankles. "You and Wally spotted a good deal. The only little fly in the ointment is now I want a piece of the action. You'll have to up your offer."

"Our proposal was quite generous."

"Not enough, Sid, baby. You're on to something. I want ten percent over my payout to the investors and five percent of the profits. Paid semiannually."

Sid hurriedly gathered up his papers.

Sipping his beer, Grady shrugged as though he didn't have a care in the world. Catching Jennifer's eye, he gave her a slow, wicked wink.

Jennifer's heart leapt into her throat. Grady had blown it. He'd asked too much. Rommerman was going to leave without falling into their trap.

Sid snapped his briefcase closed. His eyes narrowed. "You aren't kidding, are you?"

"A man has to make a living."

"All right. Six and a half percent over the initial offer and one percent on the profit. That's as high as I can go."

With a smug smile tilting his lips, Grady extended his hand. "Deal."

Looking surprised Grady had agreed so easily, Sid accepted the handshake.

Right on cue, Jake hobbled into the saloon on his crutches. He slammed up to the bar.

"I'm gonna sue! So help me, I'm gonna sue the town council, the county, the forest service, and anybody else I can think of." He slapped a newspaper down on the counter. "Somebody's gonna pay!"

Jennifer hustled over to serve Jake. "What on earth is the matter with you? Have you been drinking?"

"Not yet. But I'm gonna. Gimme a whiskey." He shook the rolled newspaper at her. "Make that a double."

"I've never seen you like this, Jake." She gurgled some Jack Daniels out of the bottle. As a rule, Jake's limit was a single beer.

He downed half the glass and grimaced. "Haven't you seen the paper? It's all there. Somebody should'a told us not to drink the water."

"The water?" she asked. Out of the corner of her eye, Jennifer noted Rommerman's interest. "What on earth is wrong with our water?"

Marty limped into the saloon with the cane he used as a prop in the melodrama. "I thought I'd find you here trying to stir up trouble." He eased himself gingerly onto the stool beside Jake. "You've got no real proof, you know."

"No proof?" Jake shouted. He thumped his fist on the paper. "It's all right here in black and white. Them fool scientists have finally figured it out. I didn't just plain break my leg. And neither did you. It's the damn water, man. Can't you read?"

"Easy now, calm yourself..."

Rommerman casually eased out of his chair. "I don't mean to intrude, but is there something in that newspaper—"

Marty snatched it away. "None of your concern, mister."

"I think it is." Rommerman wrestled the newspaper away from Marty. His eyes widened as he read the headline and then the lead article. Dots of rosy color appeared on his cheeks.

Trying not to appear overly interested, Jennifer frantically polished the counter. She knew what was in the newspaper, all six copies she'd asked the publisher to print. Based on Grady's suggestions, she'd written the article herself.

Local Water Blamed for Rash of Fractures

Scientists have identified a trace element in the drinking water as the probable cause of a rash of bone fractures suffered by local residents of Moraine.

Medical experts theorize the symptoms, which weaken bones and mimic osteoporosis, are a result of residual mercury in the ground water. Mercury was used extensively in the Sierras during the gold rush period to separate gold from ore.

Local doctors, noticing a particularly high incident of bone fractures among otherwise healthy residents, called in health experts from Sacramento. Their findings thus far are deemed preliminary.

As a result, however, local real estate agents report a flood of "for sale" listings.

One broker, who asked to remain anonymous, maintains he hasn't seen such a panic to sell since someone reported volcanic activity was possible in the Sierras.

Until studies are confirmed, scientists recommend no one, particularly the elderly who appear most susceptible, drink the water or use it for bathing.

Jennifer couldn't watch any longer without laughing. Rommerman's normally fair complexion had turned the color of a red-hot poker. His eyes were glassy. For a moment she thought he might be having a heart attack.

He whirled around to glare at Grady. "Did you know about this?" he shouted.

"I don't know what you're so upset about. There's still gold in the streams and that ought to attract—"

"You…you…" Rommerman sputtered. "You tried to trick me!"

"A deal's a deal."

Rommerman spied Grady's briefcase with the telltale corner of the newspaper sticking out. "You're a crook, Murdock. I won't stand for it. Everybody in San Francisco is going to hear about this."

Grady unfolded himself from the chair. "Let's negotiate, Sid. How 'bout three percent." He tipped his Stetson back at a rakish angle.

Rommerman threw the newspaper at Grady. "No way. I'm outta here. This deal could bankrupt me. And you can tell Wally for me not to bother to come around again. Shoulda known not to get mixed up with some wet-behind-the-ears, smart-ass kid."

Holding her breath, Jennifer watched Rommerman storm out of the saloon. The swinging doors thumped shut behind him. She choked back laughter. Tears edged down her cheeks. Her whole body shook.

When at last no one in the saloon could restrain themselves a moment longer, laughter exploded.

Grady lifted her up and twirled her around. She linked her arms around his neck and held on tight while the whole world spun, particularly her heart.

"We did it!" she cried.

"You bet we did, sweetheart. Moraine's seen the last of Sid Rommerman."

"You were wonderful. For a minute I thought you'd asked for too much and Rommerman was going to walk out. You were so sure of yourself."

"It's all those acting lessons you've been giving me."

"My hero," she sighed dramatically. She felt like Moraine had been given a second chance, due to Grady's heroics, and at an enormous financial cost to himself. How would she and the town ever pay him back? And would his success now make him feel free to return to San Francisco with a clear conscience?

Dear God, let me be able to read his mind...and his heart.

When the laughter finally quieted, Jennifer noticed Jake staring glumly at his empty glass.

"What's wrong?" she asked, puzzled. "You played your part beautifully. You were completely convincing."

"Yeah, I know." He didn't look at all happy about it. "Fact is, I'm havin' some second thoughts. Least ways, with the hotel 'n' all, I would of had some sort of a steady job. And Millie might of been able to get on the payroll doin' somethin'. We would have made out okay."

Jennifer rested her hand sympathetically on Jake's shoulder. The town's restoration had helped the local economy but not every family.

"The hotel wasn't the solution to your problem," Grady reminded Jake. "It'd be better to keep things small and build on what the town's already accomplished. Like turning Moraine Theater into a dinner theater. The ticket sales are going well, aren't they?"

"Spectacular," Jennifer replied. "I think we'll have a sellout the whole weekend."

"That's what I mean." Grady leaned against the bar. "So there've got to be other ways to bring money in here."

"Like what?" Marty asked.

"When I saw how much fun the kids had, and Jennifer told me they only spent the day, it seemed to me there ought to be a way for the youngsters to stay longer. Maybe like a summer camp."

She gnawed on her lower lip. "A hotel for kids? They wouldn't have much money to spend except on ice cream and candy."

"It's the families that have the cash to spend," Moose pointed out.

"Wait a minute!" Jennifer cried as an idea sparked. "Nyla's cabins. We could house whole families there and entertain the youngsters during the day."

"Five cabins?" Marty said skeptically.

"There could be more," Jake said. Awkwardly he swiveled on the bar stool and swung his leg around. "I've been holding on to a lot over by the mercantile for years and never knew what to do with it. If I could get a loan I could build three cabins on it. Nothin' fancy, but comfortable."

"Lots of folks around here have enough acreage to build an extra cottage," Marty agreed. He grabbed a napkin from a stack on the bar and began to jot down numbers. "Just might work, and it wouldn't change the town much."

"Most people from the city get bored sitting on the porch all day," Moose warned. "What'll we do with the adults while the kids are playing their games?"

"You'll teach them needlework!" A rush of ideas flooded through Jennifer's mind but suddenly she remembered the time. "We'll talk about this later, but now it's almost time to serve dinner and I promised Nyla I'd help. I've got to run."

"I'll go with you," Grady offered.

"I'm on my way, too," Marty announced. "I've got to share the good news. Nyla's been a bundle of nerves since all of this started."

Marty was out the door first while Jennifer said a quick goodbye to Jake and Moose.

Outside, she and Grady discovered Danny standing on the boardwalk, the center of attention among a circle of his friends.

"What have you got, Danny?" Jennifer asked, peering at the unknown object in her son's hand.

"It's a dollar, Mom. I gots a silver dollar!"

Amazed, she stared at the coin resting in her son's dirty palm. "Where did you get that?"

"Found it."

"Around here?"

"Zorro had it, Mom. In his cage." He closed his fist tightly around the coin. "I gets to keep it, don't I? Billy says finders keepers."

"I don't think…" She glanced anxiously at Grady.

With a smile, he knelt next to the boy to bring himself to eye level. "It's yours all right, son. What are you going to do with it?"

"Save it forever 'n' ever. Billy says it'll bring me lots a luck."

"Seems to me a man makes his own luck," Grady replied, using his fingers to comb away a few blond strands from the boy's face. "Luck comes from hard work, not what's in your pocket. Maybe you could put that dollar with your gold and save up for something you'd really like to have."

"We already gots a 'frigerator."

Grady chuckled. "I imagine you'll be able to think of something else to want."

The child studied Grady and then the coin. "Billy gots a neat bike with those fat wheels. He can ride as fast as the wind."

"He's much older than you are," Jennifer reminded her son.

"But if I start savin' now—"

"That's the idea, Danny." Grady tousled the boy's hair. "A very wise woman once told me money was meant to be spent, not hoarded. In fact, how about when you save up enough money maybe I could help you pick out the best bike we can find?"

"You'd put it in your calendar book?"

Grady smiled. "You bet I would. And I'd never forget an important date like that."

Jennifer's heart twisted with love at the look of adoration in Danny's eyes.

But that didn't mean Grady had made a commitment to her, she warned herself. She didn't dare lower all of her defenses again.

When they were alone on the street, Jennifer said to Grady, "You realize that silver dollar was probably yours, don't you? Zorro must have found it and brought it back to his cage."

"It's possible."

"But it was your lucky piece and you just let Danny have it as though it didn't mean anything to you."

Grady slipped his arm possessively around her waist. "It doesn't. Not anymore. Right now I'm only interested in how well that black, lacy thingamajig looks on you."

She swallowed hard. "Now? I promised Nyla—"

He headed them off in the direction of his cabin. "Looks like you're going to be late."

Chapter Fifteen

Nyla stood against the wall of the theater, her face pale, her eyes glazed. Her mouth worked soundlessly. She appeared totally unaware of all the hustle and bustle of dinner preparations going on around her.

Anxiety clutched at Jennifer. Was her aunt having a stroke?

"What's wrong?" Jennifer took her aunt's hand. Her fingers were cold and limp. "Nyla! What is it? What hurts? Can you sit down? Talk to me, Aunt Nyla!" A spasm of fear gripped Jennifer's heart.

Nyla's eyelids fluttered. Slowly she focused on her niece.

"I'm fine, dear," she replied in a dreamy voice. "How are you?"

"Scared to death about you. Why are you just standing here?"

"After what Marty said, I didn't know what else to do."

Jennifer frowned. Her aunt wasn't behaving at all normally. She led Nyla a few steps to a chair and asked someone to bring a glass of water.

"Just rest a minute," she urged, "and then you'll feel better."

"No. I think this is just about as good as a woman can feel."

"We're all very happy Rommerman has given up on Moraine," Jennifer acknowledged. By the general enthusiasm in the room, she was sure Marty had already spread the word that Moraine was safe.

Nyla smiled angelically. "Yes, Marty told us all about that. I've never seen him so excited."

"But why would that upset you so?" And send her into a catatonic stupor, as best Jennifer could tell. Maybe she ought to call an ambulance.

"It's been a long time between proposals," Nyla said simply.

Jennifer's jaw dropped open. She sank onto the chair next to her aunt. "Marty proposed?" Accepting a glass from their neighbor, Jennifer downed half the water herself.

"Wasn't that sweet of him, dear?"

"After all these years...I mean, he finally...I never thought..."

"Neither did I." Nyla sighed. "He said he'd been meaning to ask for ages but hadn't found just the right moment. I do believe he was so excited about Rommerman he just sort of blurted it out."

"But he did mean it?"

"Oh, yes, dear. He mentioned something about a honeymoon on a cruise ship. Then he kissed me." She patted her cheek as though touching a sacred spot.

"And you accepted?"

Nyla tilted her head quizzically. "You know, dear, I'm not sure. For a few moments there, my mind went quite blank."

Laughing, Jennifer hugged her aunt. "That must have been some kiss!" The surge of love and happiness she felt for Nyla nearly burst in her chest.

The older woman giggled like a teenager. "Sexiest man I know." She drew a quick breath. "You don't think Marty will make me give up writing those greeting card verses, do you? I do enjoy it so."

"He wouldn't dare."

"No, I suppose he wouldn't." She smiled, her eyes glistening with devilment. "Not if he knows what's good for him. I don't think he could handle another dose of my sweet peach delight."

They held to each other tightly, cheeks brushing together, tears of joy mixing as they laughed.

Only later, after helping to serve dinner to a full house at the theater, and when she had settled down to put on her stage makeup, did the full impact of the day strike Jennifer.

Nyla was finally going to have all of the happiness she so richly deserved with the man she had loved for years. The thought brought renewed tears to Jennifer's eyes, and she quickly wiped them away so they wouldn't damage her makeup.

Marriage. Husband. Wife. The words had such a joyous ring it was like a church bell pealing across the mountaintops.

So much happiness in one day was almost more than a body could stand, she thought, her hand trembling as she tried to quiet her emotions.

With a smile she recalled what Grady had accomplished that afternoon by blocking Rommerman's effort to take over the town. He'd risked his financial future. He might have downplayed the cost but she knew the truth. The amount of money involved was staggering to a working mother on a schoolteacher's salary.

More than that, Grady had made himself an integral part of Moraine. Jake and Marty and everyone else in the town had given him their trust. Grady hadn't failed them.

Her judgment of Grady had been too quick and far too harsh. Everyone deserved a second chance.

Why hadn't she been able to see more clearly until now just how much she'd learned to love Grady?

With his wicked eyes and sexy mustache, the villain had arrived in town to steal her heart.

With a steadfastness that surprised her, Jennifer knew she wanted to be Grady's wife. Anything less would be beautiful but have no more substance than the reflection of towering peaks in a quiet mountain lake.

If Nyla could overcome heartbreak and finally catch her man, so could she. Jennifer wasn't willing to spend ten years of her life waiting for Grady to realize what was right.

Thoughts of being Grady's wife were still skittering through her mind when she took her place onstage.

Her breath caught in her throat when he entered on cue. She knew she'd be able to see his lean, hard body and the beautifully sculpted lines of his face every day for the rest of her life and still find something new to admire.

Though she spoke her lines expertly, she felt the urgency to be Grady's wife racing through her with increasing intensity, like a windblown fire consuming a forest. She'd always been a determined person when she set her mind to a task. Tonight was no exception.

As Candice, she humbly beseeched her drunken father and pleaded with her mother to spare her from the evil Pierre. When the script required it, she managed to find shelter in the arms of Jack Trueheart, the hero.

But in her heart, Grady was the only hero she wanted.

Afraid she would slip out of character, she tried to force her thoughts into a quiet niche. They returned insistently, like a warming spring to snow-covered mountains after a long winter.

The audience cheered the hero, sighed for the heroine and roundly booed Pierre.

Pierre burst onto the stage to claim his bride. He swirled his cloak and twirled his mustache to a chorus of boos and hisses.

"Ah, you cannot escape your fate, dear heart," he said. His baritone voice seeped seductively through her pores. "To protect your family, you will be my wife."

She swooned as scripted, and Grady caught her, not the evil Pierre. His eyes were too loving, his smile too tender, for a villainous lecher.

Slowly, he lowered his mouth to cross hers.

She responded eagerly, not as Candice but with her heart. Her tongue skimmed an excited path across the seam of his lips. He trembled as he opened to her gentle penetration and she felt a power she'd never before experienced. He tasted of sweetness and love. She hungered for his flavor as though it were the only sustenance she would ever need.

He took the initiative, drawing her deeper into the kiss and giving as fully as he had received. He plundered her mouth, swamping her senses, making her forget where she was.

As though intruding from some other world, Jennifer was vaguely aware of hoots and whistles. She blocked them from her mind. Only Grady, the determined movement of his mouth on hers, was important.

Finally Grady released her from his embrace.

"Yes, I'll marry you," she said hoarsely.

A shocked expression crossed his face.

In unison, the audience drew an astonished gasp.

What was wrong? she wondered dimly. He'd proposed and she'd accepted. Why did he look so strange? And what were those other sounds that tugged at the edge of her awareness?

"Pssst," Marty hissed. "Your line is 'No, never shall I be your wife for I love another.'"

A grin split Grady's face. Under his breath he said, "I hope you meant what you just said because I've got a whole lot of witnesses."

"I thought . . . I was thinking . . ." Lord, what had she done? She struggled to get back into her role. Her line. What was her next line?

"Hark, now, villainous Pierre," hero Jack cried, ad-libbing, "you must not lead this innocent girl down your evil path."

"You're wrong, young Jack." Grady took Jennifer's hand and tenderly kissed her palm. "I am no longer a villain, for this young girl, with all of her innocence and sweetness, has reformed me. Never again will I foreclose on poor, wretched souls like you. She has taught me that money has no real meaning in life. My heart is overfull with gratitude and love." He looped his arm around her waist, pulling her close. "She shall be mine."

The audience cheered Pierre.

"And my heart brimeth over with love for you, dearest Pierre," she acknowledged for all to hear.

Another cheer.

"Wait a minute," Jack protested. "I'm supposed to get the girl."

The crowd hissed.

Pierre twirled his mustache and wiggled his eyebrows. "Get your own, kid. This one's mine."

Howling with laughter, the audience applauded as Grady dragged Jennifer off the stage. Confused, she stumbled along after him. Her head seemed to be spinning out of control.

The crowd continued to hoot and holler, but Grady forced Jennifer into a dark corner behind the drapes, kissing her hungrily.

"Shouldn't we go back onstage for a curtain call?" she asked breathlessly when he finally released her. Weak-kneed, she rested her head at the bend of his neck, feeling his pulse match her own throbbing heart. What craziness had overtaken them?

"I'm never going to let you out of my reach. I couldn't care less about the audience tonight."

"We certainly gave them a surprise ending for a melodrama." She'd made a fool of herself onstage but the audience didn't seem to mind. She could still hear scattered laughter as the crowd exited the theater.

"You almost threw me for a loop. I had to do some mighty fast ad-libbing."

"I don't know what I was thinking..." She didn't want Grady to feel she was forcing the issue too soon. It might frighten him off. It would be better for now to let him believe she'd simply made a mistake rather than have him know how desperately she wanted his proposal to be real. "It must have been the excitement of the afternoon, Rommerman, and then Marty proposing to Nyla. I guess I wasn't concentrating on my lines."

His dark eyebrows formed a double arch. "You're not going to back out on me now, are you?"

"Back out?"

"I've got an attorney friend who'd love to handle a breach-of-contract case like this. I've got two hundred witnesses. You haven't got a prayer of winning against those kinds of odds."

"What are you talking about? What happened on-stage—"

"I proposed and you accepted."

"I'm not going to hold you to that. It was only make-believe." Wasn't it? Her heart tripped a little faster.

"Ah, my precocious pretty, you don't seem to understand. I hold the mortgages on Moraine," he reminded her with a wicked gleam in his eyes. "If you don't marry me, I could still foreclose."

"You wouldn't."

"Do you want to take that risk?" he teased.

"I thought— We really haven't known each other very long." Why was she arguing? Marrying Grady was just what she wanted, and the sooner the better, as far as she was concerned.

"When you agreed to marry me onstage, I knew, right then, that's what I wanted, too."

"You're serious?"

"My instincts have never failed me, Jen. I love you. I've never been more sure of anything in my life."

It was all happening so fast. The ancient floor of the theater seemed to shift beneath her feet. Feeling as though she'd fallen under some magic spell, she clung to Grady's muscular arms for fear reality might intrude.

"There are some things you ought to know. Marty says he wants to retire and he offered me the job as bank president. But I turned him down. In time, Wally will be the right man for that job. I want to move and start a business of my own."

"Wherever you are, in San Francisco or on the moon, I want to be with you. I love you, Grady."

Her words sent a surge of elation through Grady. He hadn't been sure just where he rated compared to Moraine, and now he knew. It made him feel invincible. But her willingness to make a sacrifice to be with him wasn't necessary. He was already a convert to the town of Moraine.

"I'm good at what I do, Jenny, and I like my work," he admitted. "But Murdock Investments is my father's creation, not mine. I want to start an investment company right here in the mountains."

Her beautiful blue eyes widened in amazement, and it tickled Grady to see how pleased she was. "Probably with an office in Sonora," he said, "but that's not very far away."

"Unless you take the forest service road." She kissed him lightly on the cheek.

"That ol' beaver would miss me if I didn't check up on her at least once a week. And then stop by Edelman's for a little ice cream."

Jennifer's light laughter wrapped itself around his heart. If he could ever figure out how to bottle the sensation, it'd be an investment worth a lifetime of work.

"And now, my precocious pretty..." He twirled the tip of his mustache and his eyes narrowed with evil intent. "I'm going to take you back to my cabin."

"But why, kind sir, would you want to do a thing like that?" she asked with a none-too-innocent twinkle in her eye.

He laughed villainously. "Since you can't pay the rent, dear heart, I plan to ravish your sweet little body. All night long."

Where do you find hot Texas nights, smooth Texas charm and dangerously sexy cowboys?

DEEP IN THE HEART

Wedding Bells—Texas Style!

Even a Boston blue blood needs a Texas education. Ranch owner J. T. McKinney is handsome, strong, opinionated and totally charming. And he is determined to marry beautiful Bostonian Cynthia Page. However, the couple soon discovers a Texas cattleman's idea of marriage differs greatly from a New England career woman's!

CRYSTAL CREEK reverberates with the exciting rhythm of Texas. Each story features the rugged individuals who live and love in the Lone Star State. And each one ends with the same invitation...

Y'ALL COME BACK...REAL SOON!

Don't miss *DEEP IN THE HEART* by Barbara Kaye. Available in March wherever Harlequin books are sold.

OFFICIAL RULES • MILLION DOLLAR BIG BUCKS SWEEPSTAKES
NO PURCHASE OR OBLIGATION NECESSARY TO ENTER

To enter, follow the directions published. **ALTERNATE MEANS OF ENTRY:** Hand print your name and address on a 3″×5″ card and mail to either: Harlequin "Big Bucks," 3010 Walden Ave., P.O. Box 1867, Buffalo, NY 14269-1867, or Harlequin "Big Bucks," P.O. Box 609, Fort Erie, Ontario L2A 5X3, and we will assign your Sweepstakes numbers. (Limit: one entry per envelope.) For eligibility, entries must be received no later than March 31, 1994. No responsibility is assumed for lost, late or misdirected entries.

Upon receipt of entry, Sweepstakes numbers will be assigned. To determine winners, Sweepstakes numbers will be compared against a list of randomly preselected prizewinning numbers. In the event all prizes are not claimed via the return of prizewinning numbers, random drawings will be held from among all other entries received to award unclaimed prizes.

Prizewinners will be determined no later than May 30, 1994. Selection of winning numbers and random drawings are under the supervision of D.L. Blair, Inc., an independent judging organization, whose decisions are final. One prize to a family or organization. No substitution will be made for any prize, except as offered. Taxes and duties on all prizes are the sole responsibility of winners. Winners will be notified by mail. Chances of winning are determined by the number of entries distributed and received.

Sweepstakes open to persons 18 years of age or older, except employees and immediate family members of Torstar Corporation, D.L. Blair, Inc., their affiliates, subsidiaries and all other agencies, entities and persons connected with the use, marketing or conduct of this Sweepstakes. All applicable laws and regulations apply. Sweepstakes offer void wherever prohibited by law. Any litigation within the province of Quebec respecting the conduct and awarding of a prize in this Sweepstakes must be submitted to the Régies des Loteries et Courses du Quebec. In order to win a prize, residents of Canada will be required to correctly answer a time-limited arithmetical skill-testing question. Values of all prizes are in U.S. currency.

Winners of major prizes will be obligated to sign and return an affidavit of eligibility and release of liability within 30 days of notification. In the event of non-compliance within this time period, prize may be awarded to an alternate winner. Any prize or prize notification returned as undeliverable will result in the awarding of that prize to an alternate winner. By acceptance of their prize, winners consent to use of their names, photographs or other likenesses for purposes of advertising, trade and promotion on behalf of Torstar Corporation without further compensation, unless prohibited by law.

This Sweepstakes is presented by Torstar Corporation, its subsidiaries and affiliates in conjunction with book, merchandise and/or product offerings. Prizes are as follows: Grand Prize—$1,000,000 (payable at $33,333.33 a year for 30 years). First through Sixth Prizes may be presented in different creative executions, each with the following approximate values: First Prize—$35,000; Second Prize—$10,000; 2 Third Prizes—$5,000 each; 5 Fourth Prizes—$1,000 each; 10 Fifth Prizes—$250 each; 1,000 Sixth Prizes—$100 each. Prizewinners will have the opportunity of selecting any prize offered for that level. A travel-prize option, if offered and selected by winner, must be completed within 12 months of selection and is subject to hotel and flight accommodations availability. Torstar Corporation may present this Sweepstakes utilizing names other than Million Dollar Sweepstakes. For a current list of all prize options offered within prize levels and all names the Sweepstakes may utilize, send a self-addressed, stamped envelope (WA residents need not affix return postage) to: Million Dollar Sweepstakes Prize Options/Names, P.O. Box 4710, Blair, NE 68009.

The Extra Bonus Prize will be awarded in a random drawing to be conducted no later than May 30, 1994 from among all entries received. To qualify, entries must be received by March 31, 1994 and comply with published directions. No purchase necessary. For complete rules, send a self-addressed, stamped envelope (WA residents need not affix return postage) to: Extra Bonus Prize Rules, P.O. Box 4600, Blair, NE 68009.

For a list of prizewinners (available after July 31, 1994) send a separate, stamped, self-addressed envelope to: Million Dollar Sweepstakes Winners, P.O. Box 4728, Blair, NE 68009.

SWP-H393

HAPPY VALENTINE'S DAY

James Rafferty had only forty-eight hours, and he wanted to make the most of them.... Helen Emerson had never had a Valentine's Day like this before!

Celebrate this special day for lovers, with a very special book from American Romance!

#473 ONE MORE VALENTINE
by Anne Stuart

Next month, Anne Stuart and American Romance have a delightful Valentine's Day surprise in store just for you. All the passion, drama—even a touch of mystery—you expect from this award-winning author.

Don't miss American Romance
#473 ONE MORE VALENTINE!

Also look for Anne Stuart's short story, "Saints Alive," in Harlequin's MY VALENTINE 1993 collection.

HARVAL